T0159049

THE KARMA CHRONICLES
PART 1

HADRIAN'S SEAL

PEPPER CARLSON

BALBOA.
PRESS

A DIVISION OF HAY HOUSE

Balboa Press books may be ordered through booksellers or by contacting:

Balboa Press
A Division of Hay House
1663 Liberty Drive
Bloomington, IN 47403
www.balboapress.com
1 (877) 407-4847

Because of the dynamic nature of the Internet, any web addresses or
links contained in this book may have changed since publication and
may no longer be valid. The views expressed in this work are solely those
of the author and do not necessarily reflect the views of the publisher,
and the publisher hereby disclaims any responsibility for them.

The author of this book does not dispense medical advice or prescribe the use
of any technique as a form of treatment for physical, emotional, or medical
problems without the advice of a physician, either directly or indirectly. The
intent of the author is only to offer information of a general nature to help
you in your quest for emotional and spiritual well-being. In the event you use
any of the information in this book for yourself, which is your constitutional
right, the author and the publisher assume no responsibility for your actions.

Any people depicted in stock imagery provided by Thinkstock are models,
and such images are being used for illustrative purposes only.
Certain stock imagery © Thinkstock.

Print information available on the last page.

ISBN: 978-1-5043-7264-0 (sc)
ISBN: 978-1-5043-7263-3 (hc)
ISBN: 978-1-5043-7265-7 (e)

Library of Congress Control Number: 2016921295

Balboa Press rev. date: 01/18/2017

ACKNOWLEDGEMENTS AND GRATITUDE

Thank *you* for being curious about this book. May you find it compelling and may it inspire you in your own individual way.

Special thank you to Howard Wills for giving me permission to use him, his words, his teachings and his prayers in my story. Thank you Howard for the gifts you share with the world. I am honored to be able to include you, your words and some of your prayers in this story and the two that will follow. Thank you. May we all find our way to the *Light*. You can experience Howard Wills and his prayers at http://www.howardwills.com.

Very special thanks to Barbara Klein-Carey for being a mom to me for the past 20 years of my life. I count my blessings everyday for your constant and endless words of encouragement. Thank you for believing in me, even when I didn't believe in myself.

Thank you to everyone I have ever met and come across, for every author of every book I read that helped arouse me from my slumber.

Thank you to my Guardian Angels that chose me as a conduit of hope and inspiration. I am also grateful for the opportunities and the feedback the Universe keeps sending my way. It's taught me that letting go isn't falling.

CONTENTS

Prologue
One Hundred Years Ago

The grand baroque-style ballroom had to be over six thousand square feet. The off-white vaulted ceilings were covered in great detail by cherubs in various displays of recreation. Some looked to be dancing barely covered by beautiful intricate flower bands around their waists. The flowers were so bright and detailed you could almost smell their fragrance filling the room. Some of the little cherubs were depicted as cupids flying around as if they were searching for an unsuspecting lover at whom they could shoot their arrows. My favorites were the quiet ones with their eyes closed, small hints of a smile on their lips, and their hands clasped together, fingertips brushing against their chins. I couldn't help but wonder what they were praying for.

The mirrored columns and crystal chandeliers rounded out the beautiful room in such a way that the varied work areas didn't seem out of place like they should have—nor did the five angelic beings hovering around a long reclaimed wooden table. I noticed the elaborate and delicate large tree etched into the wood, covering the entire length of the top of this glorious table. The leaves even seemed to move with the breeze coming from the open windows.

"Am I dreaming?" I must have asked out loud because, as

if on cue, all five of them glanced in my direction with what I perceived to be looks of disdain as I carefully stepped closer to my dragon, Cireath.

"So it is true," spoke the one they called Archangel Gabriel, the revealer who helps you understand visions of the future, and it was directed toward Cireath.

"Yes," Cireath answered. "The terms have been accepted by the Order of the Dragons and the Keepers of the Realm. Lord Hadrian is here to sign the scroll of destiny and to understand the energetic capacity of when karma meets fate."

It was Archangel Michael, the protector and one of great valor and strength, who spoke next. "Then let it be known here now, in the seen and unseen, that the energy shift to take place will be new to us all, and may the blessings of God and all the Beings of Light be upon us."

Archangel Uriel, the keeper of wisdom and patron of the arts, stepped forward, pulling out a very long scroll from inside his cloak. He moved forward to the wood table, beckoning with a nod for Lord Hadrian to follow as he let the scroll untwist over the table for all to see. Lord Hadrian stepped forward with Cireath as they both began to read:

> Lord Hadrian, let it be known that energy changes between us in unspoken lessons of the past. Our ancestors, the first in each line, set our course by their actions and reactions sending them forth through the ages by example and repetition. With time, these transferences became habits, and it will be hard to sever the ties. The proof that some lineages skip a generation but still reside in the DNA is evident within you. You have fallen prey to the ways of those who came before you.

With every action will always come reaction, and these hold great consequences.

Your immoral acts were dishonorable, and for your sins against humanity will come a bounty with no monetary price tag.

You will not be whom you used to be, and you cannot go back to holding life's proverbial hand. Your new life will give you opportunities to be accountable. We hope that you learn to recognize when something is familiar, so you don't repeat those habitual patterns. We pray that you are born anew, and this time, choose to go into the light, be of the light, and live in the light. Your past will be foreign to you but also familiar.

Your emotional responses are programmed, destined, and wired to react in a way that is based on the stories you grew up in. You will have challenges you cannot even imagine.

The way you react toward the things that happen around you (or to you) will be a sign of where you are on this personal journey at any given moment. You will seek a path to emotional intelligence and gain some momentum for karma in the realm of cosmic law.

Let it be known, karma is hereditary. Emotional or physical genetics carried down from your ancestors will be your greatest battle, even more so than it was in the battle you lost in this life. This philosophy is bred from the theories of nature versus nurture. You won't remember any of this at first, but it may come to you at some time or any moment in any future far from now.

Lord Hadrian, the time has come for your intent to meet up with your past actions. You have broken the law of moral causation, and your actions have warranted the consequences come back on you tenfold from this life, from previous lives, and from the life you are about to enter.

Let it be known and acknowledged that you waive your rights to partake in the established karmic debt plan and forfeit the seven lifetimes to pay it back. Your course for repayment has been reset on a new vibrational level and is full of energetic consequence. Your moral compass must adhere to where the past meets the future.

You hereby acknowledge and are in acceptance of the consequences that you forfeit your right to the seven-year life span of the universal karmic debt repayment plan.

Signed and sealed,
Lord Hadrian

Chapter 1

To Be or Not to Be

I find myself part of a story in this life that is seven times bigger than I am. I'm pretty sure someone, somewhere, in a faraway place and very long ago, stole time. This caused a shift in the karmic debt payment plan structure that should have taken the seven years like it was supposed to.

This narrative started when I died, but I learned that the story started long before any of us ever came to be. I'm what you would call a *doppelgänger*.

A doppelgänger is a palpable double of a person in culture, folklore, and fiction. In colloquial language, the word doppelgänger has come to refer to a person's double or look-alike. In Norse mythology, we are perceived as a ghostly double who precedes a living person and is seen carrying out his or her actions in advance. You may commonly know this as déjà vu. The literal translation of doppelgänger is *double walker*, or in common English, a twin. That's me. The Twin.

While we were separated at birth by death, I wasn't the cause of the disarray of the affairs; our parents—and their parents before them and their parents before them—were going back through the various tests of time. And here now in this moment on this day, I feel compelled to tell the story because I got out, and she got left behind.

After spending a long nine months in each other's arms, overhearing the downward spiral of the world we were about to enter, I just knew I wasn't going to make it. The accusations were fierce, and the desolation pumping through our Genius Mother's veins was suffocating. There could only be enough breath for one of us, and I knew my twin was the stronger one. As much as I knew that my time to live would be taken from me, somehow I understood that my never knowing life would be necessary for my twin to fulfill her life's purpose.

It happened quickly and painlessly. I had a vision of lying in the gutter. I could feel the dirty, musty water against my face, and I could smell every bad thing that would ever happen to me wafting out of that water. I tried to wiggle free but couldn't move. Riveted to the images that played out before me, I saw a life that wasn't mine teaching me everything I would need to know. I watched myself grow in stature and knowledge to be a female with the human age of thirty-five, and somehow I knew that would be my age for all eternity. I also knew instinctively that the Genius Mother they called Paige who was trying to give birth on the table below was passing her intelligence to me as she quietly realized she was successful in letting me go from this world.

As all the genetic, energetic, and intellectual knowledge seeped inward into and through the strands of my DNA, there was a prolonged silence that seemed to wrap itself around me like a spider spinning silk around a fly. I wasn't even sure when I stopped breathing, so I gave in to that moment of paralysis and to whatever higher power would take me. In a silent whisper, I truly and unconditionally prayed to be redeemed for giving up, but I mostly prayed for my Twin, who was about to surprise everyone.

I could see the relief sweep over Paige's face as she settled back onto the table. She knew I was gone—and she seemed pleased with herself—but as the next wave of pain swept across her face, she realized I hadn't been alone, and this she hadn't counted on. From this place of higher consciousness I was able to see that my Twin would become the archetype of misplaced youth. She was about to go from the seat of neglect to the throne of unbridled chaos, and the odds would most certainly be against her. I also saw that she would be unwavering in her quest to make sense of her world, and the indelible footprints of her questioning would leave her intent on finding a way to sever the umbilical cord. It was perfectly clear that I had to find a way to help her.

The answer came promptly and plainly, since with my last breath came the gift of ageless wisdom and divine intelligence. I was now a Doppelgänger Being with vocabulary and knowledge. I had understanding and emotion and perception and intellect, and my intellect was telling me I had to send for reinforcements.

I would need assistance in a big way. I needed angels—and I don't mean just any kind of angels. I mean guardian angels of archangel proportions—the kind of angels that you only ever read about. I had no sooner thought this when they appeared to me. Like the dream team they were, five celestial angelic angels appeared, eager and curious. If I didn't know any better, I would have said they knew this was coming. Is that even possible? With no time to waste, I explained the severity of the situation. The angels assured me they knew all about it, and they had known all along they would be called upon. They quickly introduced themselves.

"I am Archangel Michael, a great prince who stands up for children. I symbolize protection, and I have great strength and valor. I am a protector from one's own fears."

"Archangel Gabriel at your service," he said, giving a playful bow as he did. "I am the revealer who helps you understand visions of the future. I am also proud to be the supreme messenger of God and enjoy overseeing communications."

"I am Archangel Raphael, and I am a healer and the guardian of the people. It is my responsibility to bring God's healing light to earth. And this is Archangel Zadkiel. He is the compassionate and merciful one. He helps heal painful memories and assists you in forgiving."

"How do you do?" asked the one named Zadkiel.

Coming forward a little clumsily with a bunch of scrolls in his hands, he said, "I am Archangel Uriel. I am the angel of the divine presence. My scrolls and books hold much wisdom. I am a patron of the arts. I like to call myself the angel of poetry."

It was Archangel Michael who spoke next. "We have been waiting patiently for the death of the Doppelgänger that would be the spiritual link to the Twin they will call Kate. We knew you would be coming, and we have been listening for your call for quite some time. You must know there are rules. You cannot interfere. There will be times when you will want to turn your head and cover your eyes, so just do it. Look away and trust that we will hold her through the most arduous times. Be prepared that in your connection with her there will be times when you feel what she feels, and it won't feel good. There will be times you will want to grab her and take cover, but you won't be able to. Also know there will be many times when she will know laughter, but that isn't what this story is about."

When they told me this, I had no idea what they meant, but boy, would I learn soon enough; they so weren't kidding.

Using poetry as a conduit and dreams as their couriers, their messages to Kate were far from ambiguous. Throughout her evolution, the poetry sent to her by Archangel Uriel would speak of the possibilities of rising above it all, but she wouldn't know enough. Regrettably, poets write from a place of anguish, so my little Kate would have to succumb to the never-ending invitations of do or die.

Young, naïve, and lost in the self-pity of the process, she would not understand the lessons their words were trying to teach. At the guidance of Archangel Uriel, it seems only fitting that I include the poems here— unscathed, intertwined in her story, and dated by human age. And so I watched as Archangel Uriel opened one of his many scrolls and whispered the first of many poems in Kate's ear.

What do you do when you wake from a dream and you're crying? The tears of a life unattended, a missed encore, a curtain call—the orchestra is a sight for sore eyes and a mystery wink. You will not look back in sorrow or in pain; look to the future and how bright it is. You will take one step at a time. You will love and prosper. Be wise in your decisions, and count your blessings. Let us, your Guardian Angels, the Archangels of Heaven itself, show you how to walk. Greet every day with love in your heart. Listen to your life and heed its suggestions, prompts, and warnings. We will assist you. We will never leave your side. Listen well to your heart, your body, and your soul; our messages will reside there. We shall help you set out to break the lineage of your past.

—Just Born

At my last breath—and even with the help of the archangels— Kate came into this world being what you might call really bad timing. She was the almost-wasn't, and believe you me, sometimes she was going to wish that she wasn't … but so it was to be.

One of the perks of my being a Doppelgänger Being hovering

in another realm, so to speak, was that it gave me more than just knowledge; I was able to read the ancient scrolls of the angels, and this is where I found the history of how my twin, Kate, came to be in this life and from this lineage. As I read, it came to life before me in images like a hologram. This I knew was Archangel Gabriel's doing.

Kate was the second born to a Genius Mother named Paige who was the daughter of Mateo, a Puerto Rican naval officer, and Sofía, a debutante southern belle from North Carolina. Paige was cute, chubby, and a child genius. When Paige was younger, she skipped grades in school, tested off the charts, and was misunderstood by her parents, who had no schooling. Sofía, draped in her mink shawl, would ridicule her for being overweight, and when it was time for scolding, Mateo would send a belt across her bottom. She was rebellious, bored, and wise beyond her years.

"Mateo," Sofía would call out in her southern drawl. "Do something about Paige! We have the veterans' ball in a month's time, and she'll be the fattest kid in the room."

I watched Paige sneaking snacks in the kitchen while Sofía, the Debutante Southern Belle, sat in the living room, cigarette dangling from her mouth, reading magazines or diet books— anything that she thought would make her daughter thinner. While in the other room, Paige would guilefully tiptoe across the kitchen linoleum to take a cookie from the jar above the refrigerator, a treat that any child should indulge in after school. It wouldn't take long for her to get caught. A smudge of chocolate on her upper lip, telltale crumbs on the front of her pristine school uniform, or an empty slot in the cookie tin would appear— all indications of her deceit, and punishment would not be far behind.

Deep down, Paige knew her father wasn't intentionally cruel; violence was just a method his generation understood. He was pragmatic and militaristic to the core. He knew he could whip new recruits into shape, and if that method was good enough for the Navy, then it was good enough for his child. She did not begrudge him his belief system. Even still, on the days she was caught, I could hear Paige talking to her doll, allowing the tears to fall slowly down her cheeks. "It's not that they don't love me. They don't understand me, and they can't love me the way I need them to. They don't know that stringent diets and physical punishment just push me further into the confines of my own mind. There's too much information in here for me. Isn't there anyone who can understand me?"

I could see Paige sitting in her room, staring out the window and watching the clouds morph into familiar shapes. She fiddled with the hemline of her skirt so much so that one area became worn down and frayed. Her mind seemed to wander, and her thoughts took her to a time when she would no longer feel the scorn of Sofía judging her waist size or to a time when Mateo would no longer swing his belt across her bottom.

Paige was now of high school age as I contemplated what this all meant, and she began to set every curve on every test and gain the respect of her high school teachers.

"Paige, come stand in for the hour while I go to the teachers' associations meeting. Cover chapter seven."

I could feel the reluctance but also a sense of pride from her as I watched her slowly approach the front of the room and begin to ask the questions of her classmates to insure they had read the chapter.

I watched Paige get home each afternoon and go straight to her room to grab her doll and stare out the window. The daydreaming seemed to act as a surrogate for the sort of love she so desperately longed for. And that is perhaps why Paige fell in love when she did.

At thirteen, Paige was on a slow walk to grab some milk at her mother's request when a boy stepped in her way.

"You again," he said with a smirk. "I have been watching for you every day for a week wondering when you'll be going to the store again," said the sixteen-year-old street kid from an affluent Cuban family who had nothing better to do. "What is your name, my vision of loveliness? I am Alex," he said.

"Umm, hi. I'm Paige," she replied, stumbling over her words.

"May I walk with you?" he asked.

"Yes, umm, okay. I'm just going right here," she said.

"Well, I will wait and walk you home then," he replied quickly with confidence.

The next morning was Sunday, and instead of going to church, she went to the corner of 185th and Amsterdam to fall in love—and for every Sunday after that as the years passed quickly, the baby fat started to melt away, and she blossomed into a lovely young woman.

This love gave Paige the drive to start working at the local hospital the day she turned sixteen, and the money she earned from cleaning dirty bed sheets got stashed under her pillow. "It may be gross, but I will have enough money to move into my first apartment the day I turn eighteen, and that is fast approaching," she said to the always-listening ears of her beloved doll.

A year later, Alex moved in, and when Paige was twenty they had Mia, their first born and at twenty-one, their second—my twin, Kate.

In that first apartment, Paige really came into her own. She was a perfect five-feet-nine inches tall with long straight brown hair parted in the middle and chocolate-cherry brown eyes. She wore a purely lit spiritual aura that she didn't know she had and still carried the hopes of childhood dreams.

One day, while Mia slept and before Kate was ever a thought,

Paige was sitting and cutting out images from magazines and taping them to the off-white walls when Alex came through the door. "I spy a beautiful woman," he said with a smile, sitting down next to her on the green velvet sofa.

Paige was talking excitedly. "This is where we will go for summer months."

Mateo was the same height, with brown hair and brown eyes too, but his eyes held more longing and restlessness. And Paige didn't notice.

"And we'll be together forever," she continued. "And we'll live in the country when we get old and maybe have some horses."

He would laugh at her, because the story was different every time.

"I thought you said we would move to Florida to be near the beach?" he would ask.

"Perhaps," she would say, staring off for a while at the avocado-green refrigerator in the kitchen, as if recalibrating the dream. "The only thing I'm sure of is that we'll be together forever."

It's one thing to be fed by daydreams and fairy tales when you're young. But in a real relationship, there are complications.

There was a lot of confusion surrounding the knowledge of my Twin's attendance. By the time she made her presence known, the future between Mateo and Paige had grown bleak. The argument was always the same. "That baby is not mine! I wasn't even here. I was in the county jail!" he yelled for the hundredth time in five months. With her fists clenched at her sides, her voice breaking over the lump swelling in her throat, Paige whispered, "Yes, she is, you crazy son of a bitch. Where else did she come from?"

Holes in the drywall from enraged fists stared back at her. Glasses lay in piles on the floor, shattered like the dreams she used to cling to. Her nose ran, and her face was streaked with tears. The

9

apartment that once symbolized a hope for a beautiful future and freedom from her family had become an empty cave.

Paige had no intention of bringing another child into the world, not when her world was crumbling down around her. When the abortion attempts were unsuccessful …

"Wait! What? Archangel Michael! Are you there?" I called out in desperation.

"I'm here, child," came his strong and resonant voice.

"Am I reading this right? Is that what happened to me? That's why Paige thinks the abortion was unsuccessful? Only one of us died, and she didn't know there were two of us?"

"Yes. What happened to you was deliberate and necessary, like we've tried to explain to you. We need you with us to be our link, our connection to the one who holds your bloodline. There is something bigger than all of us at play here, and in time all will be revealed."

With a new added slump in my shoulders I rolled up the scroll, put it neatly on the shelf, and sat back down as Archangel Gabriel opened the portal to connect me to Kate's soul.

"It is time to face the reality of the life Kate is going to live, isn't it? And you're telling me I am the link to her salvation?"

"Yes," responded Archangel Michael and Archangel Gabriel in unison.

I watched as Paige resigned herself to her new fate. Paige wouldn't turn to the parents, who would still help her even though she couldn't wait to get away from them. She wouldn't turn to her sister, Janis, a singer who was out traveling the world. Janis was four years her junior and an unexpected addition in Paige's world. She didn't have Paige's intelligence, but she had other talents. She was beautiful, thin, and tall like their father, Mateo. She had the voice of an angel, as he and Sofía were always quick to tell the

The Karma Chronicles Part 1

whole neighborhood. She was the lead in every play and went on to singing back-up vocals to some really big name performers.

Left alone to face the night, Paige would turn inward to herself and her unexpected plight. Alex, now twenty-four, had more on his mind than a wife, a kid, and another one on the way. He found solace with some street punks and at the bottom of many whiskey bottles. Drunk and slurring their words, they discovered first cocaine and then the need for the money to pay for more. Stealing money from people's homes satisfied these needs. Things could only get worse. I couldn't help but call on Archangel Gabriel, stat!

"Gabriel, why can't we help Paige? How do we just sit idle like this when helping her would help Kate? Wouldn't it? I mean, honestly, what could Kate possibly have done in a past life to deserve this?"

His response was sympathetic. "That is very observant of you, but you know I can't answer that. Nor can we interfere in a way that would alter her path. We must have faith that with our assistance, she will be strong enough to rise above all that is to come. Time will tell, and patience will be our friend."

"Okay, okay. If you say so, but it sure does feel like we have our work cut out for us," I said, my shoulders hunched even further in defeat.

"That we do. But don't despair. You must keep the faith above all else, as you are connected to her, and through you she will know hope," he replied, with a soothing pat on my back. I couldn't help but wish he could pat Kate on the back like that.

By the time Kate was two, she had taken up permanent residence in her playpen while Alex had taken up temporary residence in the county jail.

Kate slept through the nights, while Paige cried herself to

sleep over the visits to see Alex and how things had gone the day he returned to the apartment on the third floor.

It was in sleep that I watched the angels cradle her and her memories. I couldn't help but think it could have been my fault, although the angels assured me it wasn't. But still I silently wondered. Could she really feel me, them, all of us always watching over her? God, I hoped so.

Though I couldn't directly intervene in her life, and the angels had more power to communicate with her, I watched over her the way a parent would. I wanted nothing more than to protect her from the world that I had been able to escape. So while I existed with the Archangels, their comforts enveloping me like a baby kangaroo in her mama's pouch, I tried to reach out to Kate, to shield her from pain. I would find myself failing often, but I had to believe she knew we were all there.

There was so much yelling, followed by the relentless accusations from Alex. He was blinded by the paranoia of the drugs and couldn't see through his glassy eyes that Paige's heart would never know another.

The hatred in their voices felt like it was breaking every bone in my body. I could not dispel the sounds of sorrow and despair that had become Paige's voice any more than I could keep Kate from hearing it. We watched Paige wilt, suffocated by the weeds, thick and coarse, growing around her like a headdress of thorns. Her once long, beautiful, shiny hair hadn't seen a brush in ages. Her eyes had become hollow. One summer night while the rain danced around the humidity, Paige sat quietly in the kitchen feeding Mia and Kate Spanish rice and beans. Mia sat close to Kate, holding her hand while Kate looked up at her in awe.

"I think Mia is trying to protect Kate," I said to the Angels. "I can feel it."

But my words and the silence in the kitchen were quickly

interrupted when the front door slammed opened and shut, and Alex went into the bathroom and locked the door. Paige grabbed Mia and Kate, putting Mia in her bed in her room and Kate in her playpen.

As she rounded around away from the playpen, it was Alex's drunken face that met her. "You cheating, lying bitch. You ruined my life!" he yelled.

Paige couldn't defend herself. She stopped fighting back. But being greeted with only her vacant stare infuriated Alex more than her words ever could, so he resorted to what he saw on the street.

From the confines of her playpen, Kate winced at the sound of the first slap and the scream that followed. She heard the furniture breaking and the sounds of fresh wounds. She heard the sound of hair being pulled from Paige's head and saw the blood gushing from her eye. She heard Alex's final blow to Paige's right eye before she heard her limp body fall to the floor.

These are the sounds that Kate would associate with family. It was in those formative years—when most children hear the sound of their mothers cooing a lullaby or their fathers telling them how much they love them—that my dear little sister heard only violence. She had no frame of reference for love. The angels and I tried to help as much as we could. There was no way they could fill Alex's heart so full of love that he would stop. He wasn't why they were there. But they could watch over Kate and send words of love and encouragement.

On this particular day, we all watched, rapt with attention, as Alex, drunk and brazen, followed Paige into the kitchen. He swiped his hand so hard across her face that she momentarily lost consciousness. She fell hard against the kitchen floor, her skull seeming to bounce off the linoleum.

It was then that Alex turned his attention to my Twin back in her playpen. "I don't know why she even kept you," he said, more to himself than to her. Kate wasn't old enough to fully comprehend the meaning of his words. But the cold feeling began in her heart and continued through the rest of her, filling her stomach and radiating out to her limbs. It was slowly overtaking her.

I could feel it too, to some extent. But I knew she was receiving the brunt of it and knew that I could never fathom how lost, cold, and unloved she felt at that moment.

Sensing her distress, Archangel Michael was the one who sent out a rallying cry.

Archangel Raphael led the five angels as they focused their energies on her and whispered in her ear over and over:

> We call on the healing light of God.
> We envelop you in this light's facade.
> Our little one we hold in prayer,
> Please don't fret our love we share.
> Feel our guidance and this appeal,
> Know we have you in warmth and steel.
> You are in our care.

Slowly, their words began to warm her. "It's working! It's working!" I yelled, jumping up and down with admiration and respect. "I can actually feel her body temperature rising, and that impending feeling of doom is subsiding!" I knew Kate wasn't old enough to put into words how she was feeling, but Archangel Zadkiel assured me, "When the time comes and she looks back on it, she will realize she wasn't alone."

Paige stood up as Alex shifted his attention from my sister back to the fight. He pummeled Paige as if she were a punching bag. "Argh!" I whispered under my breath, covering my eyes.

While Kate feigned sleep, she couldn't help but shiver with fear as the door slammed shut behind the exiting father. The quiet game that followed stretched time to its limits. Roused completely from the drowsiness, Kate peeked through the mesh openings of her playpen. Paige, motionless and barely breathing, lay in a pool of her own blood.

Waiting in her crib for the now watered-down milk, Kate would be witness to this recurring nightmare. Sometimes Alex's beatings were worse than others. Sometimes Kate thought Paige would never get up. Sometimes she was happy to have her lying on the floor next to her because it was the closest they ever got.

I tried to focus on the link the Archangels insisted I had with my little twin sister Kate, and I tried to sing their words into her as a lullaby.

> We call on the healing light of God.
> We envelop you in this light's facade.
> Our little one we hold in prayer,
> Please don't fret our love we share.
> Feel our guidance and this appeal,
> Know we have you in warmth and steel.
> You are in our care.

I wished more than anything in the world that she could hear me. And that night when Paige finished changing Kate's diaper, I was so distracted by my own thoughts that I didn't realize my magical little Twin Kate was deep in a dream, and she had taken me with her.

It was early morning as the sun rose to meet us, and with it came a view like nothing I had ever seen before. We were surrounded by water, and we were standing on sand as white and sparkling as diamonds. Taking in every detail, I turned in place. The sky's blue was almost purple, and a bridge of alabaster stone came into view. Just beyond its opening was a land so green and lush, with well-manicured tall trees and colorful flowers in full bloom. And just beyond all this extravagant beauty stood a castle as grand as an Irish fairy tale fortress.

"Where are we?" I whispered in wonderment.

As if on cue and to my amazement, I heard, "Cireath! Slow down!" yelled from somewhere above my head. I looked up and then ducked as a dragon headed straight for me with someone riding on his back.

I opened my eyes at the same time as Kate back in the apartment on the third floor. It was quiet as I sat staring into space, wondering what that dream could mean. But around me, I saw evidence that time had passed.

Alex had been kicked out and new locks put on the door of the apartment on the third floor. But Alex knew how to get into apartments without a key. He would climb up the fire escape and in through the window to rob Paige of whatever she had left.

He would push her to the ground, empty her wallet, and swiftly kick her in the ribs before departing. Desperation made him more violent. These visits left Paige broken like the shattered glass around her. By the time Kate was four, she knew nothing of being held or coddled. She knew a lot about yelling, crying, and long periods of silence.

The angels and I were good at keeping her distracted. I would see spheres of lights brightening her room while she slept, and I knew Archangel Raphael was sending healing light to envelop her. We all worked together diligently to strengthen our spiritual connection. We showered her with love and protected her from the shadows with prayers of light as best we could.

> Archangel Michael protect the front of her,
> Archangel Raphael protect the left,
> Archangel Uriel protect the right of her,
> Archangel Gabriel protect her back,

Archangel Zadkiel, protect her from above and
below,
Angel lights combine into a powerful glow.
Cover Kate in a personal sphere,
Where love and empowerment is loud and clear.

The Archangels' lullabies comforted her. I tried to help as best
I could while waiting to visit her in her dreams again.

Archangel Michael told her stories of strength in battle;
Archangel Gabriel sent her imagery of a hopeful future.
Archangel Raphael sent the healing light of God as often as he
could. Archangel Zadkiel shielded her from painful memories,
and Archangel Uriel spoke to her of wishes and dreams through
poetry and literature.

It was their warmth—and I would like to think mine, too—
that kept her going.

As time passed and Alex and Paige grew older, Alex spent many
more nights in jail. Alex's influential family forced a meeting to
let him know he had to get his shit together or he would take his
last breath from behind bars. His uncle was the one to speak, "We
made arrangements with the DA: You are to make your choice.
Join the Military or stay in jail. Which will it be?" Alex looked
to his mother but she wouldn't look at him. With a long sigh he
said, "I'll join the military."

There were some civil exchanges between Alex and Paige. A
lot of apologies were spoken and a lot of promises made.

Shortly after he signed the enlistment papers, Alex took Mia
and Kate to the Ringling Bros. and Barnum & Bailey Circus. It
had it all—death-defying acts and women twirling batons, bicycle
riding, and elephants!

During the cab ride home, Kate and Mia carried on about
everything they had seen. They wanted to remember every detail

and couldn't wait to tell Paige. She would never believe what they had experienced, and they couldn't wait to show her their new toys.

When the taxi pulled up to the curb, Paige was waiting for them across the street in front of their building. In the chaos of speaking over each other and showing the toys that Alex had bought for them, I felt Kate hold her breath for a second too long.

It would always strike me as the strangest feeling when her heart would sink. It was the same gut feeling as when she left her favorite teddy bear on the A train and watched the doors close and the train pull out of the station, away from her. The feeling of impending doom was back, and it was unmistakable.

I watched helplessly as she turned slowly on the little heels of her navy-blue Mary Jane's and looked up into the streetlight to where Alex should have been standing. But he was gone, leaving shadows dancing on the side of the building.

They had arranged it, planned it for weeks. Alex was gone and Paige was left with her resentments, wounds and two girls to raise on her own.

The trauma of the abandonment left Kate bereft with grief, as she thought, *He left me. He left me with this woman who resents the very air I breathe. How could he do that? How could he leave me like this? He was mean to Paige, but he didn't hate me like she does.* As she looked up into the face of the Genius Mother, she saw the fear looking back at her.

"Okay. Does anyone else find this confusing?" I asked the angels.

It was Archangel Zadkiel who spoke. "It seems confusing on the surface, but try to think of this from Kate's perspective. She doesn't know a mother's love. She only senses the resentment and hatred emanating from Paige's core. Her innate intuition is telling her the lesser of the two evils is Alex because he has never physically harmed her. Nor does he emit emotions of hatred or resentment toward her. It's almost as if her body is telling her he is neutral to her, and so to her that is the safest choice."

"Oh, brother", I said, "That makes sense, and I don't like it one bit."

The shadows grew taller like an upright grizzly hovering over Kate wrapping her in its dark grasp. Kate tried to hold onto the light of the trip to the circus. She tried to smile, to recall the feeling she had felt when the archangels filled her with their love and their light. She clung to her toy, a cheap plastic thing that was made in China.

Paige looked down at her, the dusky shadows darkening her features and giving her a truly sinister glow. Her eyes were hollow, as if she were dead. Her lip curled in disgust.

She grabbed Kate by the scruff of her neck and led her daughters back to the apartment, where they were now a family of three.

After Kate and Mia were sent to their rooms and Paige disappeared to her own room and closed the door, Archangel Uriel appeared with his scrolls, opened one, and began to fill the page with ink.

Farewell to arms for forever and a day. A pairing of the heart and things are cold. A mistaken identity and a demolition. The blood runs hot and the tingling is unbearable. Time to leave. To turn our heads from what will never be. A memory under lock and key. under lock and key. You lose people along the way; you lose yourself if only for a day. The hills of distant lands are longing, and your heart beats fast. Time changes momentarily, and you never get it back. Words ring in your ears, and you're never sorry for it. That time heals all wounds seems unlikely. Sobriety of the eyes, and you fight for your composure, for where you were before this started. To say good-bye could be a hello later, but for now it is only this. There are no hellos in sight. Only shadows from the trees. You're at a loss for words. It's all very clear. Our eyes see what they want to see, and our hearts play their own music. A quiet tempo in D. So deep-rooted and raspy, so guttural and withdrawn. So lonely and so far away. So there can be no violins. Enjoy your dark blue trident and try to forget. Things are finally so clear. You're taking leave. Farewell now. Farewell to arms for forever and a day. Farewell for now.

—Age 4

Chapter 2
A Proverbial Childhood

In the first years of Kate's life she would have her first run-in with the proverbial statistics list. She was a neglected child. Paige was unable to provide the necessities for a healthy emotional life or the love and encouragement a child needs to truly blossom.

There were days when Kate would wake up, not because it was time to get out of bed, but because the walls screamed their silence at her ears. She would rise to find that there was nothing for breakfast and that Paige would not pay attention to her. Many days were spent seated in the corner of her little bedroom—not playing with toys like a normal child would—but sitting with her knees pulled up to her chest, a measure she found would stop her stomach from growling so loudly.

She had seen many shows on PBS about learning the alphabet and counting. She tried to find those shows whenever she could, but she knew that she would need more than just a TV to become smart. And even when she couldn't find *Sesame Street* on the TV, she would notice the small children in the commercials on the other channels. Their hair was brushed nicely, their clothes were clean and new, and they were always in the company of what appeared to be a loving parent.

Looking ahead, I could see the consequences that would come

from neglect and see the long-term effects weaving deep into Kate's psyche. The vibration of her low self-esteem, attention disorder, and physical injuries were enough to get the best of me. I begged the angels to call for reinforcements as Kate's name was permanently engraving itself on each new scroll of data.

As if it couldn't be any worse, Paige harbored resentments. Not only did she have the wounds of physical assault, verbal abuse, and abandonment but she also had my Twin, and she often told her, "You are nothing but a walking, breathing reminder of everything that went wrong in my life, and every time I see you or hear your voice, I cringe."

Needless to say, the years to follow were empty for Kate. The unscrupulous and unstable conflict of her world torn apart caused an emotional earthquake. Left to her own devices, she could barely hear the angels through the rumbling, which made for some very deep cracks in her foundation.

She waited to see if Alex would come back for her. He didn't.

With Mia away at kindergarten, Paige spent all of her time in her room and left Kate to fend for herself. The angels tried to help me reach her, to let her know she wasn't alone. Sometimes we were successful, and other times she just couldn't hear us. But we would never give up.

I went to see the archangels in the other realm to ask them about their plan and what we were going to do if we couldn't reach Kate to save her. As I approached, I could hear their voices coming from a room down a long hallway, and I could have sworn I heard Archangel Michael saying something about a lord and his dragon. *Huh?* I thought as I approached the door. The five of them were huddled around a table in deep conversation, and as I came into the room, they fell silent.

I opened my mouth to speak, but before any words could escape, Archangel Raphael spoke one lonely and frustrating word:

"Patience." And with that, they were gone from the table. I sat down hard in the chair as my legs gave out from under me. Staring off into space, I wondered what the heck they were talking about and if I'd really heard what I thought I did. It seemed familiar for some reason. I don't know how long I sat there trying to make sense of it, but my thoughts were interrupted by my Twin's feelings of loneliness.

Paige wanted nothing to do with Kate. She couldn't even look at her.

Sometimes Kate wondered if Paige knew she was there at all. There was nothing for them to say to each other. Kate would tiptoe into Paige's room each time with a different offer, "Mom, do you want to color in my coloring book with me? It might cheer you up." She would ask in her precious little voice.

"Go watch TV. Leave me alone. And close the door on your way out," Paige would respond, clearly going through some tough times herself.

Once in a while the phone would ring and Kate would run to pick up the receiver. Her grandfather Mateo would keep her ears full of stories and remind her that it was almost Saturday, and she and Mia would come spend the night with him and Sofía. This gave little Kate something to look forward to.

Occasionally, Paige would have to make her presence known. One time while Kate was watching television and eating her peanut butter and jelly sandwich, she needed more milk. When she jumped off the chair, a thumbtack that she had dropped earlier pierced her skin and went straight into her foot. She started wailing instantly and called out to Paige, "Ow! I have a thumbtack in my foot! Help!" After what seemed like an eternity of silence, she waited, holding her breath, for Paige to run to her rescue, and she heard Paige call out from her room, "Just pull it out!" So she did.

Though she seemed absent most of the time, Paige was still as strict as her Puerto Rican naval officer father had been with her. She imposed rules, chores, and regulations. Like Paige's parents before her, love was expressed through tangible items. The house's outward appearance was always spotless and presentable, asking the unspoken question, "What will the neighbors think?"

By the time it was Kate's turn to join kindergarten, Paige emerged temporarily from her tunnel. She became actively involved in their lives. She would walk Mia and Kate to school every morning. She joined the PTA, and she helped with the school plays. In those years, the family seemed close, but it wouldn't be long before Paige would be lost to them again.

When Kate was in the fourth grade, she wrote her first documentary about what is now known as Castle Village, which was once upon a time a real castle standing guard over the Hudson River. Kate found the son of the man who owned the original castle, and he loaned her old black-and-white pictures of the grounds. With the help of Archangel Uriel to be sure, my Twin wrote her story around the history of the castle, and she won a contest that landed her on the *Big Apple Minute*. There was no way she was going to be on TV by herself, so she recruited her best friend to be on the show with her. They had been inseparable since kindergarten, so Jack agreed to do it. They taped it in a studio, put Kate's words on a teleprompter, and filmed their little segment. But no one in her family watched it or ever even mentioned it.

Despite her family's indifference, nothing could stop Kate's love for school (also probably Archangel Uriel's doing). Every day, she would go to that brightly lit classroom and work as hard as she could. She loved the positive comments she received from her teachers, and they truly enjoyed her presence in the class. She would sit at her little desk, her nametag taped securely to the front.

All of her notebooks and pencils were immaculately organized under the hinged lid, and though other students were careless with their crayons—often scribbling off the page and onto the surface of their desk—Kate kept her desk top as clean as it had been the day she was assigned the seat. Her pencils were always sharpened. She never spilled glue. She made the highest grade on every spelling test, and all her classmates wondered how she could be so perfect.

Through the angels' encouragement, Kate showed signs of being creative, talented, and bright.

She was placed in a weekly class for talented and gifted children. The only attention she ever received was when she had to write a one-page paper asking a genie for a wish.

Dear Genie in a Bottle,

If you could please find my dad so he can come and take me away from here. I'm really lonely and he is the only one who can save me. He is either in Puerto Rico or maybe Cuba. I'm not really sure where he is, but could just find him? That's my wish.

Sincerely,
Kate

The unintended result was that the letter prompted the principal to meet with Paige, followed by Kate being pulled from the class for gifted students—the one place where she was getting any encouragement—thereby tipping the scales in the wrong direction.

They had since moved out of the apartment on the third floor and into a two-bedroom on the first floor with windows facing out to the street and at street level. But change doesn't always mean growth. With an emotionally unavailable Genius Mother and an older sister who was too big for her britches comes experiencing things before your time. The attention-starved Mia, with Kate at her heels, would search the streets for accomplices. Their quest for consideration unbound them to time, so they always missed curfew and were always grounded for something. They ran away a lot. And on one particularly warm day in August, Kate learned exactly where she stood with the Genius Mother, Paige.

Mia and my Twin left the apartment as quietly as they could and ran down the hall and out the front doors to freedom. As they came around the front of the building, Paige was leaning out the window in typical New York fashion. She had heard them leave and wanted to know where the hell they thought they were going. They stood there, not knowing what to do and not saying a word, when Kate blurted out, "We're leaving and we're never coming back."

There may have been a sparkle in Paige's eyes at this announcement from Kate. She directed her next words to Mia, the firstborn: "You should stay. Let her go, but you stay, and we'll be a happy family after all."

I blinked at this verbal bombshell, but Archangel Uriel was there in a flash.

> An unforgettable moment lost in space and there is no way back. The weeks pass like your childhood, and there is confusion. An endless cycle, round like the earth yet flat like the land. B flat. A black key on your piano. My own private tangents and no one knows. The cars pass quickly like the clouds, and there is so much mystery. The crosstown bus and no traffic. The lights are broken and a cup of rattling change rustles beyond the window. The past is gone, and yet

there are things that won't rest. They stay very
much alive in your mind like a restored classic
Oldsmobile.

—Age 11

They didn't run away, but after that, Mia and Kate spent as
much time away from the first-floor apartment as they could. Mia
taught my Twin how to smoke cigarettes and then pot, which I
must say I am not terribly happy about. Even the angels couldn't
stop her inevitable downward spiral. All we could do was watch
from the sidelines.

At the time, all of their friends were much happier hanging
out in the schoolyard, getting wasted, than they were in their
own homes.

Growing up on the Hudson River had its advantages. It was a
beautiful part of New York City, and Mia and Kate were fortunate
to grow up there.

All the kids had a story. They grew up near Fort Tryon Park
overlooking the Palisades in New Jersey. It was a beautiful park.
They owned it. It kept their secrets and protected them from
harm, the perfect escape. They would drink and have parties in
the park; they tried things that kids their age had no business
trying. For all, lives would be changed forever. The next great
hockey player exchanged a scholarship for a joint. The baseball
player, a career for a life behind bars.

They would all take turns on the phone, "Hey Ma, it's me
Janey. I'm sleeping at Mia and Kate's tonight." "Hey mom it's me
Mia. Kate and I are sleeping at Janey's tonight." "Dad, it's Levi.
Clark and I are sleeping over Chuck's tonight." And so on down
the row. Then, with their sleeping bags, booze, and drugs in tow,
they all walked across the George Washington Bridge, past a *Do
Not Enter* gate, and out onto the green grass cliffs of the Palisades.

That Monday, back at school, Mr. McCormick called Kate into his office. "Kate, your grades are falling. What's going on with you? Why do you seem so disconnected? You have gone from writing that documentary in the fourth grade to letting your studies and your talents fall prey to bad influences. What can I do to help?"

Rebellion, resentment, and loneliness took over all at once, "You can go to hell—that's what you can do." And she stormed out of his office and right out of the building, leaving Mr. McCormick to stare after her with genuine concern.

Through the years, she would be suspended for many reasons. Most of them involved misplaced anger taken out on other students.

I watched in astonishment as all the students walked through the halls to their next class, and a boy shorter than Kate said, "You're a joke" as he was about to pass her by. And before I could blink, Kate was on him in the crowd, throwing punches and trying to make contact with his face. The teachers broke it up, and Kate was sent to the dean's office again.

"Kate, I can't keep protecting you," said Mr. Herby. "The principal is sure to hear about this one, since it happened in front of everyone."

"I know, but it was his fault! He called me a joke."

"Kate, you can't let these kids bully you or provoke you. You are better than this. You have too much potential."

But the principal came into the office before Kate could respond and there it was. She was suspended for the second time that semester. "One more time, Kate, and you'll be expelled. Mark my words, dearie. We'll show no mercy," said Ms. Havenshurst. One more suspension and she would be expelled? Now I was even more worried than Mr. McCormick.

Kate was coming apart at the seams. She was even growing

apart from the once protective and reliable Mia. Coming home from school one day Kate, spotted Mia on the corner with her friends. "What are you wearing? You look like a pilgrim!" taunted Kate.

Mia turned on her with venom in her eyes. "I'm going to kick your ass when I get home," said Mia.

Kate turned and ran all the way home to get prepared for Mia's wrath. But Mia snuck up on her in the living room and when she turned around was struck in the face with the aluminum pole of the vacuum cleaner. Thinking she had killed her, Mia grabbed a bible and stuffed herself between the wall and the toilet, praying Kate was still breathing but too afraid to check.

When Paige got home, she found Kate sitting eating a sandwich. Her face had the expression of a boxer who had survived ten rounds, and Mia was trapped in the bathroom. So she did what she always did; she went to her room and shut the door.

Paige and her daughters became three strangers living under the same roof.

I watched my Twin fall farther into the abyss. I tried everything— lecturing her in her dreams, having the angels try to send messages and signs to her. But we couldn't penetrate the walls of intoxication that surrounded her.

She was wasted all the time. She was tired and she was lost. She was about to start the eighth grade. On that first day of school, she woke up not knowing how she had gotten home, how she had gotten into bed, or even how she woke up. She was scared.

During that night, the angels and I took full advantage of her delirious state by diligently bathing her in light. We sang to her and caressed her and nursed her back to life.

Not knowing how she managed to wake up but knowing it was a miracle, she blinked her eyes open as the smell of the previous nights rain reached her. Kate got herself up and headed to the bathroom to brush her teeth and get ready for school. She stood staring at herself in the bathroom mirror for what seemed like an eternity and I couldn't read her thoughts. Had something finally changed in her that morning?

My Twin went to the same grammar school for nine years with all the same teachers and all the same kids. Mr. Jackson seemed to be the only one who could get through to her, even though most of the teachers seemed compelled to protect her too. He saw my Twin's struggles, but he never judged her. He encouraged her and made a pact with her. He said, "We're going to get you focused, so you can live up to your true potential again. You strayed from your path, but you can get back on it. You can stay after school and work in the book room, and I'll help you get your grades back up so you can get into a great high school." Kate nodded her acceptance, whispering a "thank you" that was barely audible.

Then one morning, three months into the school year, Kate woke up with what she thought was an epiphany. She would leave New York. What brought her to this realization? Had she overheard a conversation? Did she have a dream that she believed was real? How could she know that her teacher's efforts to get her into a great high school would be futile? I had no idea what to think, but I suspected the angels had a plan, and I was only meant to find out on a need-to-know basis.

This feeling was unlike anything Kate had ever felt before. It was a gut feeling, something that she couldn't shake. But it was also deeper than that. She could feel it in her core, in the molecules of her bones. She was as sure about moving to California as she was sure about the sun rising. And yet, she couldn't put it into words, not because she wasn't smart enough to communicate it, but because she had no frame of reference for this sort of feeling. She just knew she would move.

I've learned a lot from the angels and the ancient scrolls I've read, and it's been written that we should be careful what we wish for; my Twin is proof that there is truth behind this age-old adage. She truly believed with all of her being that she was leaving Paige, the genius mother who couldn't love her, and the First Born, Mia, who had turned her back on her. She would be leaving everything that was familiar and taking her first plane alone across the country to stay with her aunt, Janis.

My Twin was so excited. Paige's sister, Janis, had become her idol over the years. She was fun and beautiful and well traveled, and she was a singer. She was everything my Twin wanted to be, and interestingly enough, Kate looked exactly like her. Everyone said so. "You could be her daughter," they would say. And she seemed to genuinely love my Twin. I will give her that.

Perhaps the love the Singer had for her was the one thing that Kate could wish for to keep her going. It was truly unlike anything she had ever felt before.

I remember when my Twin was a baby, whenever Janis came to visit, the first thing she would do was grab Kate from her playpen and hold her and kiss her all over her face. My Twin seemed to be the world to her. She swooned over her like a cat with her kittens. It was something Kate wasn't used to, and she wanted more of it.

Since the angels forewarned us, that the parts of the story I needed to focus on were the struggles Kate would go through, I feel compelled to give some backstory into the family gatherings that occurred over the years. Holidays and birthdays were important occasions. Paige took pride in family gatherings and came out from under her rock long enough to show the family and the neighborhood how perfect things were behind the door of the apartment on the first floor. She would spend days preparing and hours cooking, and everyone was expected to attend. There would be an apartment full of people, whether it was Christmas, Hanukkah, Easter, or birthdays. It was as if these extravagant parties would make up for all the other dreary days of the Genius Mother's life, and Mia and Kate loved the attention. With grandparents came presents. They had a closet full of toys and all the newest clothes. Grandpa Mateo spared no expense on the girls. He also showed up once a month to take Paige and the girls' grocery shopping to make sure they had food to eat.

This was the epitome of a family hiding behind the question: *What will the neighbors think?*

Even so, everyone cherished the happy days, even though someone in the family would always end up in a fight with the Debutante Southern Belle, who had an unprecedented gift for insult, and the Puerto Rican Naval Officer would have to take his wife home. It was always the same insults from Sofía and directed at Paige in what came across as jealousy. It always ended with her insisting to Mateo, "Take me home. I've had enough of this. How dare she treat me as if I was such a terrible mother." And Mateo would begrudgingly take Sofía home, not wanting to leave his daughters and granddaughters that he so often worried about.

If I indulge in some reminiscing through the memories of my Twin, I will always remember the Christmas when Kate was old enough to acknowledge how beautiful Janis was. Kate thought the light radiated from her aunt like she was an angel on top of a Christmas tree. She wore beautiful clothes, and she had an easy way with conversation. She always showed up with tons of toys and clothes for Kate and her sister. She also treated Kate as if the sun rose and set on her. Kate had never experienced anyone before who didn't have a secret agenda or who didn't greet her with immediate malice.

Janis the Singer seemed to take to her immediately, and my Twin loved it. Kate was always so happy when the Singer came and was sad whenever she left. She would dream of a life with Janis, and whenever Janis visited she spent all her time doting on Kate, telling her how pretty and smart she was and promising that some day she would take her on a trip to see the world. After all the presents were opened and the family had eaten, the Singer pulled Kate aside and handed her a bright, new silver dollar.

"Here you go, pretty girl," she said. "Always keep it with you, and it will always bring you luck!"

"Thank you," Kate replied, holding her own money in her hand for the first time ever.

"Some day you can come live with me in California," said Janis. "Won't that be fun?"

My Twin nodded like her life depended upon it. If the Singer had asked her to move that minute, she wouldn't have hesitated.

In my Twin's early years, the angels instilled in her an undeniable faith, even if she didn't know it or understand it at the time; it was woven into her DNA. Most people don't ever realize how powerful faith can be.

Shortly after the holidays, the same year Kate was in the eighth grade, a new boy moved into the neighborhood, and he pursued my Twin Kate like the Street Kid Alex had pursued Paige. Apparently, his pursuit of Kate reminded Paige of Alex, and she nearly died when the boy showed up at their house, asking to take Kate out on a date.

He was cute, and he made her laugh; he had a dark side too, and they couldn't stay away from each other. But the more they tried to see each other, the more Paige plotted against it.

One day in early March, he disappeared. No one saw or heard from him for weeks, and as rumor had it, he had come home from school one day and found his father hanging in the shower. He was sent to live with his grandmother in Kansas.

As quickly as he had disappeared, he reappeared by the end

of that April. He returned with the intention that he and Kate would spend the rest of their lives together.

Kate was only thirteen while he was eighteen, and Paige had had enough. It must have been quite the déjà vu for her! Bags packed and books in tow, the car arrived to take Kate to the hideout in the Village. It was ridiculous really, a scene right out of a *Hart to Hart* episode.

Two long weeks later (which is more like a year in teenager time), my Twin emerged from the Atrium building with their Yorkshire terrier, Joey, and walked right into him.

"Hi, Kate," he said nervously, with love in his eyes.

"Christopher, what are you doing here? How did you find me?"

"I saw Paige. I let her know that I joined the Navy and that I loved you and I needed to see you before I left. I tried to explain to her that what we have is different from what she had with Alex, because we are different from them. She told me if we both feel the same way when we are eighteen, then we could be together."

They spent hours talking and kissing each other good-bye. They didn't want the night to end, and she wanted to go with him. But she knew that he had promised Paige that he would say good-bye, and Christopher always kept his word.

The next day upon her return to the apartment on the first floor, she looked at Paige, said "Thank you, Mom," and proceeded to cry in her face.

Paige told her, "He showed up here every day, begging me to tell him where you were. We talked about his feelings and your age, and I told him that if he still felt the same way when you were eighteen, you guys could discuss it then. I don't want you to repeat the same mistakes I did."

"I know," she sobbed. He told me. But it still hurts. I'm going to miss him so much. He really cares about me."

"I know, Kate," she said almost lovingly. "Trust me. I know."

She was right. My Twin would have repeated her same patterns at the same age she had been. *Does this mean the tie to the lineage was broken?* I wondered. It sure did seem that way. Karma would prove to not be that simple. Once Christopher was gone, my Twin's determination to leave New York increased, and she became intent on putting the past behind her. She was ready to embark on the next chapter, and she couldn't get out of there fast enough.

One day shortly after Easter, Mia, now fourteen, came home and said she was moving in with her sixteen-year-old boyfriend. Paige freaked out. "You are not going anywhere! You're fourteen years old for fuck's sake. You want the neighborhood to think you're some kind of whore?" Then all of a sudden, in a slow-motion, instant-replay sort of moment, Mia slapped Paige across the face, turned, and walked out the door, taking her bags with her.

A week later, the entire family was called into Paige's psychiatrist's office. The whole family was there: the Genius Mother, the Debutante Southern Belle, the Puerto Rican Naval Officer, the Singer, the First Born, and my Twin.

Everyone crammed into the little room like a train wreck, and the psychiatrist ended her monologue with, "Paige can't cope anymore. If you don't make arrangements within your family, the state of New York will put these kids up for adoption."

Preparations were made for Mia to stay in New York with Sofía and Mateo (on paper, that is, since Mia was still living with her boyfriend and his mother in another part of town). Kate would go to California to live with Janis (who had moved to California only three months earlier), and a Christian family would act as her guardians while Janis was out on the road.

Be careful what you wish for, I thought before I could stop myself. The angels appeared, talking over each other about how the hardest parts were now set in motion and we all had to brace ourselves and be ready for what was coming. I couldn't keep up with what they were saying, but it didn't feel right, and I was at a loss considering their initial warning that I was not to interfere.

After the meeting, my Twin stormed off into the streets of New York City. She ended up at the wall at Cabrini Blvd overlooking the Hudson River where she could be alone with her thoughts and her pain. It was all so confusing for her. I could hear her thoughts so loud in my ears it was as if I were in her head. *What the hell am I so mad about? This is exactly what I wanted. Living with Janis and moving to California is what I had been dreaming of.* I looked to Archangel Gabriel who appeared at my side. "I don't understand any of this." I said with a heavy heart.

"I know", Archangel Gabriel replied, "Your twin is consumed with teenage emotions and confusions. She doesn't know what she is capable of, because she has spent these formative years without proper parental guidance. She feels alone and lost because the neglect of her childhood has rooted itself into her subconscious mind. She doesn't know that she's not alone. She only knows the life with Paige and Mia. She has grown used to it and on a deep emotional level needs to feel the way they make her feel because so far it is all she knows. Also, don't forget she is about to leave everything familiar and travel across the country by herself to the complete unknown. That might be scary for anyone. Wouldn't you say?"

Shaking my head in agreement, I asked, "Gabriel, did you know that Kate feels like she doesn't fit in anywhere? Inside, she is haunted by a notion that she was taken from the wrong family at the hospital. She honestly thinks this."

"Yes, child. We know. It is a defense mechanism she concocted to help her cope with who she is and why her mother can't love her the way she needs to be loved," he replied.

"Her thoughts are really hard to listen to sometimes, and

in some ways it is true, isn't it? She might not belong to anyone. Her thoughts can be relentless and heartbreaking, reliving all the arguments she overheard when she was a child. How does she even remember these things? It is almost as if she was well aware as far back as in the womb. Is this my fault?" I asked at the same time I realized I was rambling.

He was compassionate, letting me know they all knew what little Kate had witnessed somehow with her own ears and how the stories and fights played out in her mind like a horror show she couldn't make sense of. Her thoughts were piercing, like glass shattering against a floor. We both stopped to listen together. I realized it was Archangel Gabriel who was helping me into her mind.

"Didn't I overhear these same arguments over and over between Paige and Alex? Alex thought he was in jail when I was conceived. At the same time, somewhere on the other side of town, the Singer, Janis, was being strapped down to a table in a hospital, coming off drugs. Am I just a character in some Po Bronson novel? How do I make sense of this? If Paige, the Genius Mother, is the woman who gave birth to me, is Alex the Street Kid still my father? If Janis, the Singer, is the woman who gave birth to me, then who the hell is my father? Who knows the truth? Anyone? How many statistics lists can one person be on?" she almost screamed out loud, looking up to the heavens as the tears streamed down her face.

My Twin was still questioning herself as she made it home into her bed and started to drift off to sleep. The answer that she didn't stay awake long enough to hear was "Many."

One minute I was watching her heavy eyes take her to slumber, and the next I was viewing a beach from above. *Oh, she's dreaming again*, I thought as we swooped and dove through the air, and the now familiar beach came into view. I could see the castle in the distance and people scurrying around like little ants down below. The smell of fresh air was freeing, and the hot sun was warming to the skin. I felt my Twin lean in and hug the dragon Cireath, whispering in her ear, "You are my dragon, and I am your lord. Together we will change the world. You will help me take control, and I will rule as it is written in the scrolls. Take me down, Cireath. It's time to set things right."

I couldn't see, but the person in the dream didn't look like my Twin and certainly didn't sound like her. Then the dream took on a different hue altogether, and we were in a different time and place. The Singer Janis was with us, and this time I recognized Kate; she was crying as Janis walked away, and she woke up with a start as the alarm sounded through the quiet of the morning.

Archangel Zadkiel arrived to sit with me and watch over Kate as she woke with her thoughts already taking hold of her mind. She just couldn't quiet them. *The committee* she called them. And they never shut up.

Archangel Zadkiel was giving me some backstory to help me understand it all. He was reminding me of the events that had led to Kate's confusion. He had one of Archangel Uriel's scrolls with him as he spoke.

"Janis had always been Kate's idol, but because of her career, she wasn't around a lot. One of Kate's favorite memories was when Janis's band would present Mia and her with a huge birthday cake with sparklers on top, and they sang her 'Happy Birthday' from the stage. But there were times when the Singer was supposed to come to the house on holidays, yet she never showed. She wouldn't even call, and days would pass without anyone hearing from her. Then the call of apology would come, and Paige would always forgive her, though not until after yelling her head off through the phone first.

"I remember those calls!" I said, "It was always shortly after them that Sofía would get in a fight with Paige, and Mateo would have to take Sofía home because she would be so upset."

Archangel Zadkiel continued his story, "The scroll tells of the traumatic life of Janis the Singer, but this wasn't a part of the story you were privy to. It would seem now that it is, and it might help you understand where this is all going. Janis was four years younger than Paige. The Debutante Southern Belle, Sofía, had her when she was forty years old, which was unheard of at that time, and it was at this time that Sofía's health would start to deteriorate and she stopped leaving the house. Janis got a job running meat deliveries for the neighborhood butcher. One of those deliveries was to some sort of cult. They would use her to conduct experiments. During these so-called sessions, Janis had the emotional strength to create personalities to help her get through the ordeal. The later explanation from the psychiatrist was that she had nine different personalities, and two of them were boys. They each had their own name and were aged from five to sixteen years old."

"What?" I interrupted. "Is this for real? What is up with this family? Are they cursed?"

He ignored my outburst and continued with his story etched out on the scroll he held in his lap.

"This was during the sixties and the time of psychedelic drugs. She became addicted to drugs. It was a serious addiction, because when Kate was being born, Janis was strapped down to a bed in another part of the hospital, coming off the drugs that had taken her identity."

I stopped him. "But Kate didn't know any of this," I said. "To her, Janis was just her favorite person in the world who was going to save her from her miserable existence, and it was time for them to be a family and live happily ever after."

"That is all that is to be said on this topic for now,

Doppelgänger. We must continue with why we're here," he said and vanished.

When I looked back at my Twin, time had passed again.

As much as Kate wanted to go to California all year, once she got there she wanted to go home. She didn't know anyone. She didn't understand where she was. Pacific Palisades, California, home of the beautiful people. The rich. The famous. And Kate.

"I sure hope the angels can find her here," I said out loud, hoping they would hear me. And right on cue, I saw Archangel Uriel as he opened another one of his scrolls and start writing. As I looked down away from him in his realm I could see my Twin was writing in hers.

> One more page. One more day. And there
> is no more dancing around the merry-go-round.
> Filling space quite contrary. Her life is silent.
> There is no sound. Let the ink flow and she will
> follow you to Avalon. In the mist of tomorrow,
> singing birds hum, and no one even knows she's
> gone. A walk in silence and a landslide; where
> will it take thee? I wonder if you'll ever try to
> find me. Where's my dragon? A trampoline and
> I can't get down. Childhood memories can be so
> profound. Back and forth through times of pain.
> I'm sure I'll feel this way again. We never speak
> or laugh or sit in silence. We just yell and scream
> and invoke violence. Time to close this chapter
> and take a bow. Never forgetting that we just
> didn't know how … to love one another like a
> family should. We just abandoned the heart like
> I knew we would.
>
> —Age 13

CHAPTER 3
HERSHEY'S WITH ALMONDS

My Twin arrived on the West Coast in July of 1983. The oldest son of the Christian couple she would live with picked her up from the airport. His name was Gentry, and the minute she put eyes on him, she knew that she wouldn't fit in there either. She entered LAX with a Joan Jett haircut and a jean jacket covered in rock patches. Gentry was a blond, longhaired musician, and he talked like a character on *Square Pegs*.

Kate looked like a symbol of the East Coast, out of place among the sunshine and surfers. She could feel the sunshine on her face in a way she never had before. It wasn't the sun she was used to in New York. There was a different type of warmth to it, and it warmed her skin instantly. But it wasn't all good. There was something malicious to that warmth, and she knew that there was something about California that was going to burn.

She had never seen palm trees before, and she fell in love with them. The boy asked a lot of questions and drove like a lunatic. By the time they got to the house, she was just thankful to get out of the car. She was happy to see the Singer, but terrified to be there at all. She was brought up to her room, and when she looked out the window, all she could see was ocean. She cried.

She cried for everything that had ever happened to her. She

cried for the Genius Mother, Paige. She cried for the family she would never live with again. She cried for her loneliness and all the friends she'd left behind.

She had never been so emotionally confused in her whole life. Wasn't she supposed to be there? Wasn't she finally going to be happy there? Wasn't this California life going to be better than the life she had with Paige and Mia? She didn't know, and perhaps it was the not knowing that was making it so hard for her. To say that the move was drastic would have been an understatement. Everything was different. She felt as if someone had picked up a map of the United States by the East Coast and had shaken it until she was left hanging for dear life from a California palm tree.

She didn't want anyone to know how confused she felt. Her guardian, Darcy, wondered why she was so standoffish but just assumed it was teenage hormones; it would be best if she left my Twin to figure it all out on her own, but she couldn't help but try. She had two boys and didn't know the first thing about a teenage girl uprooted from her family.

"Kate. How are you doing? Do you want something to eat?"

"No, thank you. I'm going to walk outside," Kate replied politely as she headed out the door.

She found solace in the ocean and half-pound bars of Hershey's with Almonds. She would write poem after poem while shedding tear after tear for how lonely she was. I'm pretty sure this was Archangel Uriel's doing and was his way of comforting her and helping her work through her feelings. She was alone on a bluff with no one to answer life's questions. Janis was on the road, the guardian was at her store in the Palisades, the father was golfing, and the boys were out surfing with their high school friends.

She wasn't invited to any of it. It was the longest summer of her life. By the time school started, she was twenty pounds heavier. Janis was horrified when she returned to take Kate shopping for school clothes and supplies. She would spend the following months in matching sweat outfits and going on one expensive diet after another. But the more they tried to get my Twin on a diet, the more she would sneak food. It was a horrible cycle, and she couldn't hear the angels who were trying to get through to her. I felt our link breaking, and I was scared.

The days wore on like a silent movie with my Twin's whimpering being the only sound effects. But this movie would soon become a horror show as Janis, my Twin's idol, would be revealed one personality at a time.

I went looking for the Archangels, stat! I found them in the other realm, all watching one of Archangel Gabriel's holograms. I could have sworn I saw someone riding on a dragon with a bow and arrow in full charge, but the minute I blinked to do a double take they were all looking at me, and Archangel Gabriel had hidden the image from view.

It was Archangel Michael who spoke. "Sit down, Doppelgänger," he said. There is something you must understand in order for you to keep your strength and will about you. Human lives are cyclical, and each person in a family's line plays a part in fulfilling the karmic destiny. For every action there is a cause and the reaction that follows. We are intertwined in a karmic destiny here that is new to all of us. We must each play our part in helping your twin live out hers. We warned you in the beginning that this would not be easy. But it is necessary. Please stay strong and know that we are all in this together."

And with that, I was back in the realm of human life and didn't like what I was seeing.

It was now September in California, and my Twin was off to school with the neighborhood kids she never saw in summer.

The school itself was nothing like the six-story building she had gone to for nine years. This was a huge campus with one-story buildings that looked like a well-kept and oversized trailer park. It was middle school, so it was only three grades, but it seemed like it had enough kids to fill a high school in New York.

In homeroom she sat next to a kid who looked really familiar, but she couldn't place how. "Hey there. You're new, aren't you? I'm Brad," he said with a smile. And it was the same smile of a famous comedic actor who was one of Paige's favorites.

"Hi. I'm Kate. Yeah, I'm new. I just moved here from New York. I live with my aunt and the Alcotts on the bluffs," she said with her heavy New York accent while thinking, *Holy smokes! I'm sitting next to the son of the guy from the movie* Fatso!

"Cool accent!" he exclaimed. "You sound like my dad. And I know the Alcotts. The sons are my older brother's age. They all go to Pali together."

He introduced Kate to all his friends, more kids of famous parents who grew up very different from her.

Weeks passed, and friends came easy, trading laughs over Kate's accent. The kids used her as a character study for their drama classes that Kate wasn't allowed to partake in. She was forced by Janis to take typing instead of drama. "It's practical," she argued. "You need to be able to get a job and have skills."

"But I'm the only one not in the class. I feel so left out," my twin insisted—to a battle lost before it began.

Kate was getting used to the routine and really liked the friends she was making. Her new friend from her English class, Lily, actually lived three houses away from her on the bluff. They spent a lot of time together, and Lily showed her the ropes of the neighborhood and introduced her to another set of friends. Things seemed peaceful and almost normal until one day in late October when Kate walked into the house and was met by the sound of a crying child. She dropped her schoolbooks at the door and headed toward the kitchen. By the tone of the whimpering, the child couldn't have been more than five years old. Assuming someone's kid must be over, Kate headed toward the sniffling sounds in the kitchen. As she entered the room, she saw it was her Aunt Janis sitting at the table, bent over an unfinished bowl of cereal.

Speechless, my Twin sat down at the table as Janis looked up at her with tear-stained cheeks. Through her sobs, a distinct five-year-old's voice said, "I can't finish my cereal. I poured too much, and now I'm going to be in so much trouble. What am I going to do?"

In shock, my Twin stared back into the eyes of this woman she no longer knew and assured her, "It's going to be okay. Here give me the bowl. I'll get rid of it, and no one has to know." Janis let her take the bowl, and as she walked to the sink with tears starting to stream down her own face, the Guardian, Darcy Alcott, entered the room.

"What's going on in here? Are you okay?" she asked this version of Aunt Janis. As the five-year-old's voice filled the room again, I felt my Twin stop breathing and that familiar feeling of impending doom taking the last bit of her reality with it.

At this time, Gentry came running into the kitchen, grabbed Kate, and took her upstairs to his room.

While Kate openly sobbed and her shoulders shook, Gentry explained, "Your aunt is very sick. She has been for most of her life. It's how her and my mom met. Janis had sought guidance and help at our church. A very reputable psychiatrist that is a member of the congregation came to meet with Janis, and after days of tests and evaluations, Janis was diagnosed with multiple personality disorder. Dr. Matthews prescribed meds, and they seemed to be working. She hasn't had many episodes since she has been living here."

"What is it? What's wrong with her?" Kate whimpered in what also sounded like a kid's voice now, even to me.

He continued. "She has eight personalities, two of which are boys and a couple of which are young," he said. "They all have their own names, and while they know about each other, your aunt doesn't know about any of them."

Being a teenager and having seen *Sybil* on TV, my Twin was having none of this.

The angels were all around us, trying to strengthen our link as her relentless thoughts confused the air and her breathing came out in gasps. Her thoughts asked, *Is this really happening? What could I have possibly done in a past life to deserve all this?* Out loud she asked, "How long has my aunt been like this?"

"We think since she was just younger than you are now when it first happened," Gentry responded. He kept talking and talking for what must have been most of the hours of the night, but my Twin caught only pieces of it.

Her brain tried to make sense of what she was hearing. Her Aunt Janis had been in gay relationships, but it wasn't her; it was the personality by another name. There was a sixteen-year-old personality, and when my Twin thought deeper about this twisted fantasy, she interrupted his rambling. "Was it the sixteen-year-old who took me out in the Village to see bands play and to buy expensive clothes and shoes?" she asked with a chuckle that failed her. *Good grief,* she thought.

As for the other personalities, she had no idea, and whether it was all a plot to hide her same-sex relationships from the church, my Twin would never know.

But as the story unraveled and she looked back on the past, it all started to make sense.

Holidays and birthdays were important occasions in the family left behind in New York. The Genius Mother took pride in family gatherings and came out from under her rock long enough to show the family and the neighborhood how perfect things were behind the door of the apartment on the first floor.

She would spend days preparing and hours cooking, and everyone was expected to attend. There would be an apartment full of people, whether it was Christmas or Hanukkah or Easter or birthdays. It was as if these extravagant parties would make up for all the other dreary days of the Genius Mother's life.

Everyone cherished the happy days, even though someone in the family would always end up in a fight with the Debutante Southern Belle, who had an unprecedented gift for insult, and the Puerto Rican Naval Officer would have to take his wife home.

Looking back on it now, there were many times when the Singer wasn't present, and the family was told that she was on the road singing.

But then my Twin pondered all the times that she would hear the Genius Mother on the phone with the Singer days later. "What do you mean you can't remember where you were? I spoke to the band and you didn't have a gig. It's a holiday! It's been days, and we haven't heard from you. You missed Thanksgiving, for Christ's sake." Then the Singer would show up with mounds of presents and all would be forgiven. Did Paige know about her sister's psychotic disorder? Had she kept it a secret all these years? Did the Debutante Southern Belle and the Puerto Rican Naval Officer know what had happened to their youngest daughter, Janis? Or was everyone just in denial? Archangel Uriel appeared just in time as the etchings on a new scroll started to take shape.

A sip of water on a hot summer's day. A walk
by the river or a nap in the shade. Dances in the
shadows and silhouettes in the sand. Drum beats
in the jungle and another's helping hand. The

crescent moon's smile in a faraway place. The lullaby of an angel who has fallen from grace. Rain showers encourage life, a single flower blooms. Running through your memories and a life has ensued. Sudden artistic movements and a newborn child's laugh. Sincere affections conveyed on someone else's behalf. An Alice in Wonderland and not your typical cliché. Another sip of water on a hot summer's day.

—Age 14

One day Janis had a quarrel with the woman who owned the house in California. She was visibly upset, and she grabbed my Twin and said they needed to go for a walk. I could sense my Twin was fearful of what the Singer might say and more fearful that perhaps it wasn't really her. As they walked, Janis said, "We can't stay here. I think I'm going to move us back to our place in the Village in New York, and you can go to school there."

My Twin carefully asked, "But what will I do when you're traveling? I won't be allowed to live there by myself." Thick silence fell on them. My Twin was visibly nervous, and she didn't know how to proceed, since there was no way of knowing who she was dealing with. Though treading lightly, she saw this as an opportunity to get some answers. The memory of the confusion surrounding her birth came flooding back to her in droves: Alex accusing Paige of being with someone else, some ancient fantasy of being taken by the wrong family, and the distant memory of someone saying Paige wasn't even the woman who gave birth to her at all. And before she could stop herself, she blurted out, "Are you my real mother?" Without so much as a sideways glance and with a nonchalant flip of her hair, the Singer said, "I could be. It's possible." And then she changed the subject.

My Twin felt crushed. She wanted an answer, but she also knew she would likely never get it from Janis. Archangel Michael appeared and took my hand in his. "This is all very confusing, I know. It only gets worse. All of Kate's memories are getting jumbled up between what she thinks was said, how she remembers her birth, and the fantasies she has because she resembles her aunt so evidently."

I couldn't help but ask, "How could the Singer be so flippant with her response? Didn't she know that my Twin's identity was hanging in the balance? How could my Twin know who she was if she isn't sure who her parents are?"

Archangel Michael responded carefully, "This is a lineage that holds much confusion. I will see if Archangel Gabriel can make sense of this, but I can't make any promises. We are learning through his imagery that we have also been given limited access to information." Before I could argue this, he was gone, so I focused on what was happening before me.

Heading back toward the house as if they had never been on a walk, the silence was ringing in their ears. I could hear my Twin's thoughts as the question took shape in her mind. Looking up at her aunt through the corner of her eye, her question came through loud and clear: *I wonder who she is now.*

Back at the house, Janis went up to the guest room, and my Twin went to the kitchen to drown her confusion in food. As she shoved the last bite of the first half of her peanut butter and jelly sandwich into her mouth, she heard raised voices coming from upstairs. Then she heard her guardian, Darcy, come out of her study and her son, Gentry, yelling, and a man's crazed voice that no one recognized.

It sounded dangerous and heated. My Twin sprinted from the kitchen and through the dining room, and what she met at the foot of the stairs would be forever ingrained in her memory.

The unrecognizable voice of a horror movie villain was coming out of the Singer's mouth. The hairs on the back of everyone's neck were on full alert. I don't know what he was saying or whom he was saying it to, but the next thing I knew the doctor flew through the front door as Gentry whisked my Twin into the kitchen, where she cried like a rainstorm.

"What the fuck is going on?" she asked Gentry. "What's happening to my aunt, and what is that doctor doing to her?"

A syringe later, all was calm and quiet, and there was another family meeting. "*Now where am I going to go?*" she said so only I could hear her.

"Sick?" Kate asked Darcy, still sitting at the kitchen table an hour later. "That's your prognosis? She's fucking possessed. Is she preparing for a movie role and you forgot to tell me? When does the curtain drop for intermission?"

There was silence as the doctor came into the kitchen. Darcy shot him a look, and he said, "She's asleep. I don't know what triggered this, but I've given her new medication to keep her calm. She's wearing a ring now, and each personality has been assigned a finger."

I could see and feel the archangels surrounding my Twin, but no one else did. All of a sudden Kate started screaming at everyone in the kitchen. "You have got to be fucking kidding me!" she yelled. "Are you all mad? This is the most ridiculous bullshit I have ever heard. You people are crazy. I've spent my life with this woman, and I have never seen such crap. Nor has anyone in my family. What kind of church creates an illness to cover the fact that someone used to be gay? It's the medication that's making her sick, and all of you!"

With that proclamation, my Twin ran from the room, went up to her bedroom, and cried herself to sleep.

Her dreams were dark and dangerous with fire burning

everywhere. I could feel the heat and see the sweat glistening on my Twin's brow. She was out of breath from running. The footsteps chased her through the wildfire, and just as the hands of flames reached her, she awoke, gasping and coughing.

As the months passed, no one mentioned the circumstances surrounding that night again, and perhaps unnoticed by everyone else, Janis stopped wearing the ring. I also noticed that nothing of the sort ever happened again. Kate must have been right; this was all some weird cover-up of the fact that Janis at one time in her life was gay and had been very much in love with the woman she lived with. Sheesh.

But even so, the memories of those incidents would weigh heavily on my Kate for the rest of her life. Even as she got older, she would always view these memories through an adolescent lens and associate them forever with not knowing exactly what had gone on with this family of strangers. She would always be able to remember the fright and terror that accompanied another episode Janis was having. She would always be able to recall the uncertainty of each attack and how it seemed that her life was left hanging in the balance.

The good thing was, the kids at school saw past Kate's weight, and they had no idea what kind of life she was living. They were still infatuated with the fact that she was from New York and that she had the accent they all wanted to learn. Break dancing was new in LA, but Kate had learned it in the fourth grade, so she made more friends. Popular friends. Things were turning around.

The children of the rich and famous got into as much trouble as my Twin did back home in New York. Perhaps even more so, because in LA, everyone is spread out all over the place, and the money you took from your parents was never missed. Kate found herself submersed into a whole other set of circumstances not to be proud of. Within two months, she got caught with a joint and was given quite the lecture by Janis. As she listened silently to the Singer's expression of disappointment, I felt our link strengthen. The five archangels were all standing in the room with us, as if everyone could see them. They were collectively sending light and love and messaging her.

They chanted, "We call on the healing light of God. We envelop you in this light's facade. Our little one we hold in prayer. Please don't fret our love we share. Feel our guidance and this appeal. Know we have you in warmth and steel. You are in our care."

As if she could hear them, which I am convinced now that she could, Kate made the active decision to turn her life around and start thinking in a different direction. Shockingly, she started going to church and became actively involved in the Sunday school for kids, and she even began holding Bible study at her house once a week. She seemed happy from where I sat. There weren't any more weird episodes with Janis; she was getting along with the guardians, Darcy and her husband Drake, and her best friend became the boy who had picked her up from the airport.

Kate and Gentry would hang out in his room together after everyone went to sleep, and they would talk for hours. He would play guitar and sing to her, and she knew they fell in love on those nights together and that they would love each other for all time.

Most nights they would sit in their pajamas, reading magazines or listening to records. He was always the perfect gentleman, and she didn't need anything more from him than the attention he lavished on her. She had never felt so needed before, nor had she ever been in a relationship where she wasn't the only one who needed something from the other.

Because they were both teenagers, they could understand each other in ways the adults couldn't. They could complain about math tests, talk about songs on the radio, and wonder about what their lives would become someday. They didn't need anyone else in those moments, and simply speaking with one another brought them closer together.

Kate would always remember the night they fell asleep in each other's arms. It was such an innocent moment, and up until that point, she had never felt so loved and truly happy. They had been listening to the radio and singing along with the songs they knew. It was late, but like always, they planned to stay up and chat about everything they wanted to share with one another.

As the night wore on, they both became more and more tired. They each lay down on the floor with their heads near the speaker of the stereo, the slow vibrations of the bass in the pop song throbbing in their eardrums, even though the volume was low.

Together, they slowly began to nod off, her with her head on his chest, and he with one arm around her shoulder. It was the most love another human being had ever shown Kate. And while she loved it, she was also afraid of it.

What she didn't know was how to handle her feelings, and she had no one she could talk to about them. She became a little rebellious, pretending to keep secrets from him and trying to make him jealous. She went out with her friend Carolyn one Friday night but was vague about their plans in the hope that he would be left wondering.

"What are you guys up to tonight?" he asked as he saw her come out of the bathroom.

"Nowhere." she replied. "Just hanging out with Carolyn. Maybe Westwood."

Little did she know that that night she would get added to another statistics list. As the thought entered my mind, I saw a scroll appear at my feet. I picked it up and started reading.

On any one given day can come an unprecedented thought. It could be about that one day long ago when you played as a child, free of mind and of spirit. Or it could be when you were a teenager and poetry ruled your being and kept you sane, or when the tears fell on any given day and you didn't have anyone to give you a tissue.

—Age 14½

Chapter 4
No Crosstown Bus

After being at the arcade for most of the night, Kate, Carolyn, Billy, and Sam headed to Sam's house in the Palisades Highlands. Carolyn and Billy were in the family room getting their smooch on while Sam and Kate sat talking in the living room. Kate was getting worried for time, knowing she had to get home before midnight. Looking at her watch, she said to Sam, "I better grab Carolyn. We need to get to the bus and get back to my house. It's getting late."

"Yeah, it's getting late for all of us," he agreed.

Kate and Carolyn were at the bus stop for what seemed like forever, while Carolyn droned on about kissing Billy and how much she liked him. To Kate's horror, Carolyn suddenly looked at her watch and then said, "This is taking way to long. We need to get a ride." I could see the look of shock that covered Kate's face, but it was covered by a laugh as she assumed Carolyn was joking. But Carolyn continued, "It's fine. Don't be such a baby. Everyone in the Palisades does it. It's totally safe. I've done this a ton of times."

In New York, you grow up taking the subway, so not much scared Kate. She considered herself a street kid like her dad, Alex. But she was scared of getting into the car of a stranger. This fear had been instilled into her as a child. She could hear Paige's voice loud and clear in her mind saying "Don't take candy from strangers, and don't get into their cars."

At the bus stop, she tried to hide her apprehension. She didn't want to show Carolyn how much the idea truly terrified her. But she also didn't want to do anything that could get her killed. She wasn't interested in becoming another statistic—least of all, that kind of statistic.

Kate definitely tried to convince herself it was a joke, just another way to kill time while they waited for the bus to come. But Carolyn showed her how easy it was to just put your thumb out. They were laughing and carrying on like the school girls they were and would take turns putting their hands out, and then they would sit back on the bench or dance around it while talking about the fun night they were having.

Kate was sitting on the top part of the bench with her friend facing her when headlights suddenly illuminated the bus stop from behind.

Carolyn swung around, saw the car, and looking back at Kate she exclaimed that they had a ride. Kate was riveted to the spot, while Carolyn kept saying, "Come on, let's go. I told you we'd get a ride." And with that, she jumped in the back seat. It was all such a blur, a storm of New York intuition thundering in her brain as to how wrong all of this was. I will never forget the sounds of Kate's mumbling about how she couldn't let her friend go alone as she climbed in after her.

My Twin will forever remember the sinking feeling as she sat in a stranger's car and, to her horror, heard the sound of the doors locking automatically from the driver's side door.

There was nothing special about the car, but Kate was very uneasy. She couldn't put it into words. The glow from the car stereo was the only light, save for the light from the moon above.

The night had turned eerie, one that my Twin wouldn't soon forget.

They drove the winding roads of Sunset for what seemed like hours. They passed the high school she thought she would no longer get to go to. She became lost in her fear and bewilderment, thinking, *How the hell can I get out of this car without getting killed, or worse, getting my friend killed?*

As they came up on Via de la Paz, through the silence came my Twin's muffled, shaky voice: "You can just let us out up here. We'll walk the rest."

The man pulled into a gas station that had been closed for hours and was completely dark. He sat there as they both cried for their lives in the back seat. He then turned around in his seat and stared at them. He would stare, and then he would close his eyes again. Was he pleading with himself not to kill them? Was he contemplating letting them go? He held a knife before them as he stared some more and thought long and hard. The windows fogged around them like the steam from a shower, and my Twin started murmuring her farewell to life.

But he suddenly turned back in his seat and started driving again. He made the turn down toward the bluffs, pulled off the road, and turned to face the now utterly terrified Kate and Carolyn. They thought he was going to let them go, that he had thought himself out of whatever it was he was struggling with. But he instead said, "I'm going to let you go, but first I am going to fuck you."

The rope of stability my Twin was holding onto for dear life gave way, and she fell of the edge of sanity starting to drown in her own sobs. She wanted to drown. The sobs were coming so hard she could barely speak, but in a whisper she pleaded with him, "I am a Christian and I would never tell, and God will forgive you if you just let us go."

I don't know how many times my Twin was hit or how bad it hurt to be pulled by her hair into the front seat. He looked between her legs with a flashlight and as he forced himself on top of her, she tried to look out the window. I did everything in my power to break through the barriers separating us to try to save her. I yelled for the archangels: "Stop this! Stop this now! Please!"

But the familiar voice of Archangel Michael rang in my ears, "Remember, child, we cannot interfere." I was distracted as the eighth-grade graduation ring on my Twin's right hand cracked against the window over and over and over until he hit her again, saying to stop slapping the glass as he restrained her hand. Choking on her own sobs, she could hear Carolyn crying in the back seat. Her little friend had moved into the seat behind the front passenger seat to block the view. Hearing it must have been bad enough. Was she thinking about how she would be next?

When it was over, Kate crawled into the back seat and the man pulled Carolyn into the front seat for her turn. Kate hung her head between her legs, trying not to throw up what was left of her youth all over her naked legs.

When it was over, he drove some more instead of releasing them. He must have been contemplating if he was going to kill them or not. But they were to be the lucky ones.

Barely dressed and supporting each other, shaking and afraid, they half carried each other the four long blocks toward the smell of the ocean and it's crashing waves. When they finally descended to the bluff and turned onto the street of the Guardian's house they broke into a run. The Singer, Janis, had a gig that night, so the house would be empty. When my twin entered the house, she immediately looked for a place to hide. She had this horrible notion that he would come back for them. He would realize that they were going to tell, and he would come back and kill them like he said he would.

It was December 20th and almost Christmas, and everywhere people were having holiday parties and drinking eggnog while Carolyn dialed the number that had been left for them in case of emergency.

As the little friend dialed the numbers with a trembling hand, my Twin hid under the kitchen table. Carolyn was frantic in telling Darcy, the Guardian (apparently Aunt Janis was singing and couldn't come to the phone) what had happened. Carolyn held up the phone to my twin, and though she would later remember few words of that conversation, she would always remember the sound of the Guardian's voice when she said, "Now what have you done? I can't believe I have to interrupt your aunt's gig for this." The phone went dead, and I saw a vivid vision of my Twin thinking, *No,* wishing she had died in that car.

The grief burrowed into my heart like a rabbit into a hole. With my vision blurred by tears and my ears deaf with Kate's sobs, I hadn't even noticed all the Archangels hovering around me when Archangel Uriel started scribbling on one of his scrolls.

> Misunderstood and the lights are fading.
> Existential beliefs and mass confusion. One keeps
> the mind's inner raft afloat while the other wears
> the world's irony like a straightjacket.
>
> —Age 15

When Janis the Singer got home, she found Kate still under the table. No one could see the Archangels lights combining together covering her and the table in a sphere of protection, and they couldn't hear the Archangels praying around Kate either, but they were praying and they were now loud in my ears:

> God, for me, my family and all humanity
> throughout all time, past, present and future,

please help us all forgive each other and forgive ourselves.

Be at peace with each other and be at peace with ourselves.

Love each other and love ourselves now and forever. Please God, thank you God, amen.

We love you, God. Thank you for loving us. We love you, God. Thank you for loving us. We love you, God. Thank you for loving us. Thank you God. Amen, amen, amen.

Thank you, God. Amen.

By the time the cops arrived, she was on her bed with Janis holding her. She cried hysterically as she tried to answer their questions.

I heard Carolyn tell my Twin that it had happened to her, but sometime in the night Janis told her that Carolyn told her that it *didn't* happen to her. That's what Carolyn told the cops, too; she told them that the man hadn't raped her. She also told them that my Twin got in the car first, and they believed her. I always wondered how Carolyn could live with herself for telling such a lie. But as if on cue, the archangels voices filled my head in unison with those now familiar words "You cannot interfere."

While my Twin was taken to the hospital that night in a whirlwind of confusion, fear, and bruises, her thoughts were no different. *How could this happen? Why me? And why did Carolyn lie and say that I got in the car first? And why did she tell me that she was raped too and then tell everyone else that she wasn't?*

That night would be the last night Carolyn ever spoke to Kate. I guess guilt will do that to you. Needless to say, Kate couldn't return to school right away. She spent Christmas break at home and then some more time after that. In California, it was mandatory that Kate would have to go to six weeks of therapy. It didn't go well. In the first session, the therapist made the mistake of saying, "You can talk to me. I understand what you're going through."

"You do?" my Twin asked her with excitement. "This has happened to you?"

"No, but—" said the therapist, but it was too late. Kate stood up, turned her chair to face the bookshelves, and she never looked back or said another word. Every week she would arrive and then turn her seat to face the bookshelves, and there they would sit, in silence. Kate would later ask, "What did they think I was going to get out of talking to someone who had no idea what I am going through?"

She couldn't tell her about the flashbacks that she would have over the years. She couldn't warn her that one-minute she would be eating lunch with her friends, and the next minute she would be hiding under the table while her friends scurried for the school counselor. She couldn't say that she would be walking to class one minute and be wedged between the lockers the next, hiding, afraid, and alone while she relived over and over what had happened to her.

There was no one to tell about what was happening to her. There was no one who explained to her what a flashback even was, how real they were, and how it felt as if she were back in that car feeling like she was going to die.

Because of their lack of understanding, my Twin became "unmanageable." Every time she turned around, there was something else she had to do. She had to go to the police station and look through pages and pages of photographs of empty-looking criminals. The police took her fingerprints. They took samples of her hair. They asked her more questions.

Then the call came that they had found the car, and Kate

had to go to the police to see if she could identify it. She took one look at the car, ran up to it, pointed at the piece of paper on the floor of the back seat and said, "That has my fingerprints on it." And it did. Her Aunt Janis went with her to the preliminary hearing. The man turned out to be a serial rapist, and there were five other cases against him. My Twin was the only minor; the rest of his victims had been adults. One showed up still beaten to a pulp. He had grabbed her as she was going into her home, and he had beaten and raped her and left her for dead. It was a horrible reminder that nothing would ever be the same again.

Crying for a childhood lost and the hours pass too slow.
Where did that girl run off to? How far could she go?
No one saw her skip away, but she left a trail of tears.
Didn't anyone tell her? They'd evaporate with the years.
This is no Hansel and Gretel, so now there is no way home.
A little girl should not be wandering through this world alone.
Soon she will outgrow her shoes and the ribbons in her hair.
Won't somebody help the child who missed the county fair?
Won't somebody help the child? Doesn't anybody care?
Left to face the night alone, so separate from herself, all she
wanted was some chocolate milk and the cookies on that shelf.
Will she ever find her way again? Won't someone tell her
where she's from? The papers said she's gone for good, and
nothing can be done.
Won't somebody help the child who missed the county fair?
Won't somebody help the child? Doesn't anybody care?

—Age 15

Chapter 5

The House That Jack Built (Then Tore Down)

The days passed in a blur of a storm, and all was helpless. Our link felt broken, and I was losing hope that the archangels could put it back together. I was definitely missing something. Our efforts seemed to be lost on her; this felt hopeless. So I did the only thing I could think of. I went looking for the Archangels to get some answers and found them in the conference room.

The five archangels were just settling in at the long table. There was a large screen up on the wall and a modern day intercom with speakers on the desk. I quietly slid myself into the nearest seat, and Archangel Michael acknowledged me with a small nod as a man's image appeared on the screen. He had an ethereal aura about him as he smiled out at us. It was so genuine. "Hi, guys," he said. "I'm Howard Wills. I've been sent the message from Heaven that the time has come for you to gain some deeper understanding of why it was arranged between Heaven and the Counsel of Dragons for Lord Hadrian's karma to be a message for all humanity. I'm sorry to hear the Dragons are long gone from this world. Perhaps they will find their way back some day."

It was Archangel Gabriel who spoke.

"Howard, it is a pleasure to meet you," he said, "and we are all so grateful to gain further clarity for our mission. We have Kate's Doppelgänger with us, too, and we have been told that Kate will come to you in person many years from now. In the meantime, the insight is welcomed and it is time for all of us to hear the truth about what is happening in this human world."

With a nod and a welcoming smile toward me—and then a bow toward the Archangels—Howard began.

"Well let's dive right in then, shall we? For over six thousand years, humanity has been scourging itself, all life forms, and the earth through pollution, death, greed, hatred, jealousy, judgment, and overall ignorance. It is time for humanity to move into higher levels of intelligence, choosing life over death, by taking responsibility for all our actions, allowing ourselves to grow into the consciousness of what we are—in the image and likeness of the Infinite. We are the children of the Infinite—as we awaken to what we are and to our creative and potential realities, we move individually, globally, and universally into higher levels of intelligence. As we take responsibility for the health of our planet, all life forms, and ourselves—we become the guardians and protectors we were designed to be, reawakening the Garden of Eden for the earth, all life, and ourselves. Let us join in the creation and sharing of heaven on earth individually, globally, and universally."

Looking directly at me, he added, "What Kate is going through is based on the feelings they invoke, not the physical actions themselves—but she won't know this for some time. It will be a long time to come before she is fully introduced to these concepts, but please know she will be guided toward the path when the time comes that the Archangels are given permission to show themselves. And this time will come and all will not be for naught."

I pondered his last comments and held them dear to my heart.

The Archangels will get to show themselves? Will she know about me, too? I wondered. He continued.

"Well-being is a feeling. In your observations of Kate and her human life, have you ever heard someone say, 'I'm feeling great,' or 'I'm feeling bad'? Pay attention to the words. They are correctly spoken, pointing directly to a feeling they are experiencing in their bodies. Humans, like all life forms, are a feeling. Yes, we are intellectual and even spiritual, but we are also feeling.

"The human organism is immediately complicated with all the hundreds of body parts, bones, muscles, blood vessels, etc., not to mention the integration of the mind and feelings, and then our relationship to ourselves, others, and the rest of creation. And yet with all this complexity, when we boil it all down, everything comes back to how we are feeling. Truthfully and honestly, are we feeling good or are we feeling bad?

"There is an old saying, 'We cannot lie to ourselves. We can lie to the rest of the world and they may not know it, but we can never lie to ourselves.' And this brings us back to our feelings. If we are lying to others and/or trying to make excuses for our wrong actions, or trying to skirt issues or lie to ourselves about anything, we will begin to feel bad, inside and out—physically, mentally, emotionally, and spiritually. The simple action of speaking the truth about anything or even everything creates freedom—no weight, no burden, no pain, and no lie. Speaking the truth is a powerful remedy to stress and pain. It relieves and releases burdens and makes complete freedom available to us now. When someone asks you a question, give him or her the truth. When you ask yourself a question, give yourself the truth. It is a powerful medicine that creates freedom. Well-being is definitely a feeling, and speaking truthfully is a major action in creating inner and outer harmony.

"The native priests of Hawaii, called Kahunas, say that

thoughts are physical, alive, and have substance, even though they are invisible. Thoughts are powerful, and thoughts influence feelings. If we have negative, harmful, hurtful, or hateful thoughts, we are creating the same types of negative feelings. So very simply, the remedy is to think positive blessing, non-judgmental thoughts—simple, happy, positive thoughts. When we allow our thoughts to be simple and positive, we free ourselves of the weight, burden, and unhappiness created by negative judgmental thoughts. When we practice the art of forgiveness and positive, happy, non-judgmental thinking, we start feeling good, happy, and free. When we start feeling good, happy, and free, complete well-being in all areas of our lives will follow."

"Oh. I so look forward to Kate finding this in her life," I whispered. Archangel Zadkiel put his hand on mine with a nod of agreement.

"Remember, well-being is a feeling, and if we are honestly feeling good inside and out, then our health will be a reflective measure of our true inner feelings, in a physical way. The inner feelings are reflected in our bodies. Let us think positive, blessing thoughts and create inner and outer well-being for ourselves.

"The last thing we can talk about that affects well-being is the actions we and others take in life, the actions whereby others affect us, whereby we affect others, and whereby we affect ourselves. Action is the last leg of the triune creation process: thoughts, words, and deeds—to create the present and the future. By partaking in positive and blessing actions, we are creating blessings for everyone in our presence—and what we do to others, we do to ourselves. So by blessing others through positive actions, we are also blessing ourselves and helping ourselves to feel better and have greater well-being. Lord Hadrian wasn't privy to any of this. He followed blindly in the footsteps of one of the ancestral lines of his people. But remember that without the signed scroll of

Lord Hadrian to fix his karma, Kate would never have been born. She is lashing out and feeling misunderstood. She has already experienced things no one should ever have to go through. Being a teenager is hard enough. Being a teenager with Kate's past at only fifteen years old—and having no one who understands what she is going through—is daunting. But this is not about reasoning the events. This will be about the feelings she will one day put to these events. She is a teenager starving for attention. She has become submersed in negative love syndrome and the symptoms are too deep for anyone to understand, because of how expertly closed off she has become. She wants to be a kid with a normal life and normal family, but it's too late for that. She doesn't know her fate was set when Lord Hadrian signed that scroll a hundred years ago. The people around her don't know what to do for her because they are too busy going through their own lives in the dark unaware of what it means to truly live in the light. These feelings Kate has are hard to fathom, but know that everything she is going through is necessary for all of you to lead her to where she needs to go. As she gets older, you will help her find her way to meditation, health, and wellness—and all of us. You will see."

"Thank you Howard. This has been most insightful. We will see you again soon," said Archangel Michael.

"Yes, and keep whispering the prayers to her. They are getting through to her, and she will need them now more than ever as she gets older and her life threatens to lull her into the dark. Keep her looking toward the light at all costs. Farewell my friends. May the light of God be with you all on your quest. See you soon." And with that the screen went black.

"We should get back to Kate," I said. "She is going to need us now more than ever." Archangel Uriel grabbed my hand, and with that we were all watching the living room as Kate came through the door.

It was right before summer break as she came in, opening a letter from her sister Mia.

Dear Kate, How's it going? I have some news. For the past year I have been talking to our father. He has a wife and a son and they live in a really nice house in Las Vegas …

"Oh dear," I said, interrupting. The letter included pictures of him and his new wife and a half brother two years younger than my Twin that she didn't know she had, and I could sense the feelings of utter confusion start to seep into Kate's mind and heart.

In Mia's typical manner of speaking, Kate could sense she was bragging and showing off, as if Mia thought she was better just because she had been speaking with their father. The letter went on about receiving birthday gifts from him, of going to a county fair, and even going to a baseball game with him and his new family. My Twin sensed Mia's pride in every word of the letter and hoped beyond all hope that she would get to experience it someday too. She wanted to be the one who attended the major league baseball game. She also wanted the man who was her father to buy her a baseball cap and some popcorn. She wanted to help the little brother she didn't know she had to try to catch foul balls. She wanted to have a stepmother who doted on her and told her how cute she looked in her new baseball jersey. She wanted to go out for pizza with the family and laugh as they talked about the game.

It didn't make sense to her that this was something that her sister got to do. Why wasn't she invited? Why hadn't her father reached out to her? Did the Genius Mother not tell him that she'd left New York? Did her father know she was in California?

At first she was speechless. Then the anger hit her like a slap shot, and she threw down the letter and ran up to her room.

Face down on her pillow; she was tormented by the familiar

questions. *What the hell is going on? Who the hell am I? Who are all these people? Whose life am I living anyway?* The déjà vu echoed precariously loud in her ears.

The next day, Darcy the Guardian and her aunt Janis sat Kate down for a heart-to-heart. It was Janis who spoke. "Kate, it's been a really hard year for all of us. We don't know where you're coming from, and we each have our own set of problems to deal with. Your mood swings and disruptive behavior are more than we are equipped to handle. I will be on the road all summer, and Darcy needs to tend to her store. The good news is we spoke to your father, and they would love for you to spend the summer with them."

Finally, she felt as if she would be getting some answers. She wanted to know why he had left her life and why he had been talking to her sister. But she also just wanted him to love her, the way a father should love his child. She needed some sort of stability, and the story her sister told her in her letter about the baseball game seemed like the best sort of stability she could hope for. She so desperately wanted to be like the families on sitcoms. It was within reach; she just had to have a family first, and then everything would fall into place.

She packed her bag, much like she had when she moved from New York to California. She didn't have much that was hers—just her clothes and a few books. Everything fit easily into one bag. She knew she needed to get away from California and the hand she had been dealt while she was there. She was excited about spending the summer with her father, but she was smart enough to know that she needed to be wary. Even though she was still young, she couldn't help but feel as if everything always turned out for the worst. She had a terrible sinking feeling that visiting her father was going to be just the same.

My Twin arrived at McCarran Airport a lost, overweight and

lonely child who had seen too much and done too much for a fifteen-year-old.

Alex the Street Kid and his new family were nice enough. They were happy to have Kate, and they had a nice house and some horses—and they told funny stories.

While the Las Vegas heat was much more intense than the California sun, Kate welcomed the change. Though she expected to see the city of sin, she was greeted with a much different sight. Sure, as she landed she could see the casinos, but she was taken to quite a different world. The house was big and comfortable. It was the first time that she walked into a home and felt immediately that it could be her home.

The desert sun shone in all the windows, illuminating the house and brightening every room. The fabric on the furniture was bright and cheery, and while the house was lived in, it was still clean. It reminded her of the houses on the sitcoms she had watched on TV while the Genius Mother had locked herself in her room. It looked like the sort of place where she was supposed to grow up.

As far as she could tell, there was nothing wrong with the place. But she was still wary. She had moved all the way to California from New York only to find that her living arrangement wasn't exactly the fairy tale she assumed it would be. She tried to quash her enthusiasm and good feelings. She wanted someone to pinch her, just to make sure this wasn't a dream. I have to admit something didn't feel right to me either, but of course I would have to keep that to myself.

Her stepmother Vivian was in the kitchen cooking something that smelled delicious. Her brother sat in the living room, reading a comic book. Her father, Alex was looking at her.

She inhaled deeply, the scent of dinner warming her and making her hungry, even though she had eaten before the flight.

"I can't believe I'm here with you," my Twin said.

"We're glad you could come and stay with us," Alex replied. "It's been too long."

And just like that, the apprehensions she felt, the anxiety that seemed to fill her stomach, and all her worries melted away. She felt that she was meant to be there. And even if she was only going to be there for a summer, she was glad to have this opportunity to spend time with her father.

But I saw what my Twin missed—the feelings behind the words he spoke didn't reach his eyes.

As the summer progressed, my Twin fell right into the family routine. On Fridays, they would order pizza and play board games. Kate couldn't help but feel that she was meant to be there. She had never had as much fun as when she sat at the kitchen table with Alex, talking and laughing as she picked pepperoni off her pizza and bought property in Monopoly. She even liked spending time with Vivian, her stepmother, though she was initially stressed out about the possibility that their relationship wouldn't work. She had read Cinderella and feared the proverbial evil stepmother.

For the first time in a long time, Kate wasn't running with a bad crowd. Sure, she heard occasionally from her friends in California in phone calls and letters, but she didn't hear from them often. She was very content in Las Vegas with her family, and she tried not to think about leaving.

As it does in teenage years, summer was over faster than it began. Alex and Vivian were sitting with Kate at the table having pancakes and hash browns when Alex said between bites, "Janis called to ask if you could stay and go to school here this year. She hasn't been well, I guess, and she thinks having you with her is too much for her to handle." Kate looked from him to Vivian, and I could tell she was wondering what had really been said during that phone conversation. I did pick up the faint question that formed in her mind. *Why did this sound so familiar?* she asked herself.

It was Vivian who spoke next, "We would love it if you stayed with us." But the delivery of the statement let my Twin know she had no choice, and they sent for the rest of her things.

Everything seemed fine and normal, and her stepmother helped her enroll in school. She even took her to buy a new denim jacket and get a haircut at a nice salon.

"I'm glad you're here," Vivian said. "It's nice to have a daughter."

My Twin could feel the love swelling in her heart. "I'm glad I'm here," she said.

They became fast friends, and occasionally, when the boys in the house became too much for them, they'd get manicures together and see romantic comedies at the theater.

But my Twin couldn't stop the feeling that everything was too good to be true. She didn't feel she deserved all the nice things and experiences she was having. It was from all the years she'd spent believing that she didn't deserve nice things and all the years of hearing of her unworthiness from her guardians. And whether it was because this good thing wasn't meant to last or because it became some sort of self-fulfilling prophecy, my Twin's life was headed for another wrong turn.

I went looking for the archangels.

I thought I would find them in that conference room again and prayed to God that they wouldn't vanish when I entered the room.

But they weren't in the conference room. They were in a grand room that looked like a cross between a baroque ballroom and a modern-day architect's office.

Archangel Michael stood at the head of a long wooden table, holding a red marker, and what looked like maps covered the entire surface like a cloth. He was drawing lines from place to place and making notes as if it were some kind of timetable.

Archangel Gabriel was sitting at a table covered in what could only be described as futuristic machines and monitors. My mind registered the term *virtual reality*, but I didn't know what it meant. I could see images and colors, and Gabriel was swiping at them with his hands, moving them together and piecing them into place like a puzzle. It was quite beautiful but intimidating at the same time.

Archangel Raphael was sitting crossed-legged on a cushion in a corner with his eyes closed. A bright white light that looked like it had tiny angels dancing inside of it surrounded him. His hands were in the air, and his head was covered in luminous light prisms; the energy seemed to vibrate around him like it was alive.

Archangel Zadkiel was standing in another corner in front of a long window with velvet curtains open to the sides. He was emitting a very powerful hue of purple and white light, and he had a large ball in front of him. It looked like it could be the earth as it hovered in front of him at waist height and seemed to emit a fiery glow. If my eyes could be trusted, the light looked as if it were made of tiny words, and I strained to make them out. As the words shifted in and out of the light, I was able to decipher some of them. In different shades of purple were the words *mercy, amnesty, remission, absolution, forgiveness*, and many more.

Archangel Uriel was sitting off to the side of the grand room, perched high on a tall stool. He hovered over an artist's desk that slanted toward him and had a built-in side table in which I could see unopened scrolls and quill pens with feathers of all sizes and colors. There where ink stains everywhere below him on the floor, which went unnoticed as he wrote diligently and mercilessly. His handwriting covered the opened parchment before him with the words of encouragement and enlightenment of another one of the prayers written by Howard Wills.

Prayer For the World

God, For Me, My Family, Our Entire Lineage And All Humanity Throughout All Time, Past, Present, And Future, Please Help Us All Forgive Each Other
Forgive Ourselves, Forgive All People And All People Forgive Us Completely And Totally, Now And Forever Please God, Thank You God, Amen
Fill Us All With Your Love And Give Us All Complete Peace Now And ForeverPlease God, Thank You God, Amen
Help Us All Love Each Other And Love Ourselves Be At Peace With Each OtherAnd Be At Peace With OurselvesNow And Forever
Please God, Thank You God, Amen
God, We Give You Our Love And Thank You For Your Constant Love And BlessingsWe Appreciate And Respect All Your Creations And We Fill All Your Creations With Our Love
We Thank You, God, For Your LoveWe Thank You, God, For Our LivesWe Thank You, God, For All LifeWe Thank You, God, For All Your Creations
We Love You God. Thank You For Loving Us.
We Love You God, Thank You For Loving Us We Love You God, Thank You For Loving Us Thank You God, Amen
God, Please Open, Bless, Empower, Expand Lead, Guide, Direct And Protect Me, My Family And All Humanity Throughout All Time, Past, Present And Future Now And Forever. Please God, Thank You God, Amen Thank You God,   Amen

I didn't want to interrupt them. I wanted to sit there forever and take in everything they had to offer, hoping it would touch me, make me stronger and more capable to live up to the tasks I was being trusted with.

I felt the first tear fall down my cheek as my heart opened, and I thought I might break in two. The love, warmth, and devotion emanating from the room were almost too much to take. Couldn't we just bring my Twin here, just once? If only she could feel this firsthand and know that this brilliant and magical team of archangels were here for her and would always be here for her.

As we learned from the scrolls and Howard Wills, we couldn't stop what was happening. History had already written itself, and as the archangels kept telling me, I couldn't interfere.

It was Archangel Michael who looked up from his maps and spoke to me in a clear and concise manner. "Please do not lose faith in your connection with your Twin. You must know that people will invade her space, and you need to know that for the most part, it's not personal. It's just a way of life. The divine blinds most people, so they can't see it. They have their own karmic debt to pay but must also play the role to help others fulfill their karmic debt.

"Some people are so trapped in transferences they are blinded by it and know not what they do. Boundaries are often crossed, but she will come to know that she doesn't have to be walking around with a chain fence around her. They are tests. It's a big world out there, and your Twin is going to encounter all kinds of people and circumstances that will try to get the best of her.

"She will come to know there had always been a definite and compelling sense that she was different. She is gifted with the hope and ability to see that she must be here for some predetermined purpose, but she will always ask, 'How can one person have such tragic life experiences at such a young age?' She will always wonder what kind of karma this is. But her grasping the knowledge of karma will come later, when she's older. Now is about experiencing, and while the lessons are painful and tragic, they are still lessons. The revelations will be intense, but she won't always be scared of them.

"Eventually she will commit to the changes of the cycles and go with the flow, but for now she must experience things in this way to help her dig herself out of the rubble."

With that, I was back in the bedroom with my Twin as the boxes arrived from California and my Twin was officially moved in. She was surprised to see so many boxes, but didn't let on to Alex and Vivian. As she unpacked them quietly in her room, she learned that her aunt Janis had gone shopping. She had bought her an entire new wardrobe, writing books, and a bunch of cute knickknacks.

With her belongings came the first signs of how things were changing. But at first the changes were subtle. They would be watching TV and Vivian would be getting something from the kitchen, and Alex would say, "Let's hide."

Hiding in the closet, waiting in the dark for Vivian to come back into the room, Alex adjusted himself accordingly to put his hand on my Twin's ass.

I could feel the panic, the trepidation that stops your breath as if fear itself has put its hand over your mouth. Vivian would come into the room, and they would jump out and scare her screaming "Boo!" like life was normal and they were normal. But they weren't, and no one noticed.

The Street Kid turned out to still have a love of the bottle, and he and Jack spent a lot of time together. The daily party was rounded by the attendance of prescription medication. This all went perfectly with his penchant for gambling, which explained why there was always so much cash around. Vivian, the Half

Brother, Joey, and Kate would sit and watch him play blackjack for hours, Vivian growing more agitated and my Twin becoming more disgusted with her life.

Had he not learned anything from what happened in New York? In and out of jail, almost going away for good, and then joining the military, only to return to his roots of booze, lies, and gambling? I bet none of this was mentioned in the letters he sent to Mia. Alex, the Street Kid, was an expert manipulator.

But my twin seemed to be following in Alex's footsteps. Had she not learned anything either? My Twin still kept in touch with one of her friends from back home, which was how she learned about the cocaine the neighborhood kids found in a basement of one of their buildings hidden in huge garbage cans lined with black bags. Each bag was filled with cocaine, like in a scene from *Scarface*. I heard Kate ask, "Will it help me lose weight?" to which the friend replied, "Yes it will. If you send me fifty dollars, I could send you an eight ball of the stuff."

That night my Twin risked her life sneaking into the Street Kid's room and swiping a fifty-dollar bill from the wad of cash he'd won that night playing blackjack. She carefully sealed it in an addressed envelope and dropped it in the mailbox before anyone was the wiser.

Within a week, the package arrived. The fat envelope was decorated with drawings, and it enclosed a long letter and folded-up aluminum foil containing enough cocaine to last a lifetime.

My Twin's rich friends in the Palisades had taught her about cocaine, so she knew how to do it. And do it she did. She did a little bit every day and ate the daily minimum of required food, and with all the extra energy she started doing workouts in her room. She would do leg lifts and push-ups and jumping jacks; she was determined to get strong and in shape. Weeks passed and she was in the best shape she had ever been in. This was way less expensive than the diets the Guardian had put her on. She laughed to herself, thinking of all the money they had wasted. Those people didn't want her anyway.

Her body had begun to change. She was a completely different girl from the one who had spent days crying in her bedroom and eating Hershey's with almonds on the bluff the summer of '83. With the cocaine use and the change in her body came a boost in her confidence. Her body was starting to resemble the bodies in the magazines that she read.

But she wasn't the only one who noticed the change. At first, Vivian and Alex congratulated her for sticking to a diet and for working out. But then they became concerned. The weight was falling off so quickly that they worried she might have an eating disorder. They began to watch her closely. And at first, it seemed that maybe just her diligence and her youthful metabolism were what was making the weight drop off. But slowly they began to see that she would crash after a high. They would see her sneak off to her room. They noticed how secretive she was becoming.

But all good things must come to an end. One day when my Twin's friends were over watching movies and eating pizza, Vivian realized that Kate wasn't eating and questioned her. The half brother answered instead. "I think I know why," he told his mother, and he went to my Twin's room and retrieved the stuff from her hiding place and handed what was left to his father.

In a normal family, she would have been severely scolded and grounded for life and maybe even made to see a counselor, and the cocaine would have been flushed down the toilet. Her new family did all those things except for the latter. As part of her punishment, my Twin had to stay in the bathroom with the Street Kid while he did the rest of the cocaine and talked her ear off for what seemed like the rest of her youth.

He scolded her of course, but his words fell on deaf ears. It's nonsensical to scold a child for something the parent does himself or herself. And so my Twin didn't learn a lesson from the incident, other than that her father was a complete hypocrite. Words streamed out of his mouth, but my Twin didn't pay attention. The more cocaine he did, the faster he spoke. He talked in circles, blurring his words together. My Twin couldn't wait for it to be over.

After that, my Twin was cut off from the outside world. She was not allowed to write to her friends or take phone calls from anyone. She was not even allowed to call the Genius Mother or the First Born. She was in a cage, and there was no way out. Her only outdoor activities were when she paced around the pool, crying and howling her poetry to the heavens.

The Street Kid kept drinking, and with that came more hiding in closets so they could scare the Second Wife. She had nowhere to turn and no one who would believe her. She was trapped.

That night back in her room by herself she pulled out one of the pretty little notebooks that had come in the boxes her aunt had sent her. She started writing at the same time I watched Archangel Uriel start scribbling on his scroll. Acting as the conduit, the poem therapy continued and I couldn't help but observe that most of them seemed to flow like streams of consciousness.

Torn between two worlds I cannot reach and
with only prayer to guide me, I thirst for each.
In search of my life, I try again to figure out the
past of why and when. In search of my life, I take
the tests. To make it on my own I have bequest.
A childhood of hopes that no one knew. Once I
saw in a dream-state that most come true.

—Age 16

The sun outside was shining brightly, but my Twin was confined to her room when the phone rang with the news that a trial date had been set for her rape case. She was to be flown with one of her parents back to California and put up in a hotel overnight. The following morning she was to report to court and give her testimony.

She begged Vivian to please be the one to take her because she didn't want to be alone with Alex. She begged and pleaded enough that Vivian agreed to go with her.

Even though her bag was packed, Vivian never boarded the plane with my Twin. Instead, Alex arrived, took his seat next to the daughter he didn't think was his, and ordered himself a scotch. Five drinks later, the plane landed in Los Angeles, and they grabbed a taxi to the hotel.

Nighttime came early, and she couldn't wait to close her eyes. She longed to dream and forget about the impending day in court and her memories of that horrible night. As her head hit the pillow, she tried to remember the happy times of innocence and wonder at home when she and the First Born played with their dollhouse that their Aunt had bought for them. She focused only on whatever happy memories she could muster, shutting out the feelings of loneliness that came with the happy memories. It was Mia's smile she saw and their giggles she heard as she drifted off to sleep.

I don't know how long she slept before Alex's voice stirred her consciousness. But it was his body pushing against hers as he joined her under the covers that fully awakened her. She felt his hands on her, and her body froze. Numb from the inside out, she told him to get off.

His aggression grew and he told her the story of how she was his daughter, even though she spent most of her life being told that he thought she wasn't his daughter. But, he said, if she weren't his daughter he wouldn't just touch her like this; he would do much more. Well, thank God for small favors.

She lost it, her thoughts once again screaming in her ears, "So this is proof that I'm his daughter? What the fuck?"

She punched him and got out of her bed and went to his, saying, "You're drunk! Sleep it off. I have a big fucking day tomorrow!"

A moment passed in silence as she wondered yet again what she must have done in a past life to deserve all that was happening to her. She was barely sixteen.

The Street Kid drunkenly staggered back toward her bed, but he tripped and hit his head on the nightstand. My Twin threatened to either kill him or turn him into the police.

He must have hit his head hard and passed out because he didn't say a word or move. My Twin tiptoed over him and crawled back into bed, where she drifted off to a restless sleep while the Street Kid lay blacked out on the floor.

The next day, neither of them mentioned the previous night. As they approached the courtroom, she looked everywhere for her Aunt Janis, but she was nowhere to be found. In her place was one of the rapist's other victims, a woman whose face still showed her battle wounds as she walked by them. One of her eyes was swollen shut and her mouth was inflamed with bruises. Her face was living evidence of how hard she must have fought to unsuccessfully defend her honor.

By the time my Twin was called to the stand, she was riddled with fear and consumed by anger.

Her thoughts were wild with accusations. Was this all some ploy to diminish her spirit or make her stronger? Choosing the latter, my Twin took her seat in the witness box. She directed her gaze at the bailiff, standing between her and the accused, as he asked, "Do you so solemnly swear to tell the truth, the whole truth, and nothing but the truth, so help you God?"

"Yes, I do," she said.

The questions are a blur now, but it was unfortunate for the defense attorney that my Twin had the night that she'd had. Steadfast in her hatred, her answers never faltered, and the defense attorney was unable to sway her or divert her from the truth. It didn't matter how many times he asked a question or how many different ways he phrased it. She was unwavering.

The question came without warning: "Is the man who raped you in the courtroom today?"

"Yes," she said through one tear of fear.

"Can you show the court who that man is by pointing at him?"

My Twin turned her face slowly toward the man who had changed her life forever. She lifted her hand and pointed right at his face. He would never hurt anyone else again.

Things were different after they returned to Las Vegas. The Street Kid went on a major losing streak. First they lost the horses, then the furniture, and then the house. They moved four people and a dog into a one-bedroom apartment. The Street Kid and the Second Wife fought constantly, and they ate white rice with a fried egg on it for dinner.

The Street Kid took up sport hitting my Twin since the Half Brother was too big to hit. She was always grounded for something. One day she was out walking his precious dog and had stopped on the stoop to talk to some neighborhood kids. The dog tried pulling her to go after another dog, and unfortunately the friend who helped her happened to be still holding the leash as the Street Kid and the Second Wife came walking up the stairs. Before she could flinch, she was face down on the ground with the taste of blood on her lip. In one swift movement, the Street Kid had backhanded her in the face and grabbed the leash.

Once she was in the house, he beat her like he used to beat the Genius Mother, and he locked her in the bedroom closet. Hours went by and she was left there in the dark. She must have been praying out loud when she heard the Second Wife on the other side of the door. "Who are you talking to? No one is going to help you in there," she whispered, and she left the room.

I don't know how long my Twin was in there, but when she heard them leave the apartment, she mustered all the strength she could and somehow broke through the cheap closet door.

I am pretty sure it was the archangels who pushed open that door for her that day and sent her out to freedom.

She went out the bedroom window and headed toward the desert. She kept walking until she couldn't walk any longer. She lay down on a rock and cried herself to sleep.

I could hear my own voice yelling for the archangels as I watched the desert sun take all the moisture from Kate's body. Through my tears, I didn't see the bright white light emanating from Archangel Raphael, hovering above her, or the group of boys approaching my unconscious Twin's body.

Roused from her deep sleep by hands on her shoulders, she opened her eyes to her neighborhood friends, who had found her lying there, broken and dehydrated.

They brought her home to their Redheaded Mother, Rachelle, as if my Twin was a stray kitten left in a yard, and they begged her to let them keep her. They argued that it wasn't safe for her to go back. They promised to take care of her and keep her safe.

After much debate in their little kitchen, the doorbell rang and two uniformed officers entered. Rachelle had called the police, and Kate was taken away by the state of Nevada and put in protective custody.

"It's a long weekend, so the judge won't be in chambers until Tuesday. But you'll be perfectly comfortable and safe," they said, and they left my Twin to sign the paperwork that would put her on her fifth statistics list. She was now a number in the system.

Saturday morning, she woke to rain coming through her window and a headache from crying herself to sleep. She jumped off the top bunk and found her way to the kitchen for breakfast. It was loud and crowded and more like a school cafeteria than a kitchen. She walked the line and settled into a corner table by herself. Lost in her eggs, she didn't even realize a kid no more than eight had sat down across from her. With a cheerful, "Hi, you're new," he shoved three pieces of bacon into his mouth and smiled, barely keeping the food in.

As my Twin raised her head to greet the little voice, her eyes scanned over his burnt skin like a CAT scan. The fresh burns were red and swollen and looked as if they were covering previous burns. My Twin was mortified, but her horror went unnoticed by this magnificent creature of strength and humor. In spite of the circumstances, he was a bundle of quiet joy, questioning her about where she came from and how she was doing. As he got up to leave to tackle his morning chores, he turned quickly and said, "You're cool. Do you want to be my friend?"

To choke back the sobs that were threatening to escape Kate's soul, she just nodded as emphatically as she could, and with a smile, the boy skipped off. Kate couldn't get to her room fast enough. The tears were already streaming down her face as she climbed up to her bed. She couldn't hold on. The tears at the indecency of it all blinded her. It wasn't about her anymore. Compared to the suffering of the eight-year-old boy with the chipper disposition, her life suddenly seemed insignificant. This innocent child's Genius Mother couldn't refrain from burning him?

My Twin and the little burn victim would spend the next twenty-four hours hanging out together, playing checkers, and laughing and talking about everything except why they were there. As Sunday morning visiting hours approached, the kids all waited with bated breath for their parents to arrive.

The Burned Kid and Kate hid in the back of the crowd, not wanting to see anyone. When he spotted his mother, the tremors coming off his little frame sent Kate leaping into the air with her fist aiming straight for the woman's face. The guard lunged toward Kate and lifted her in the air like serving volleyball.

Kate was ushered back to her bunk by the head of the center who had admitted her. "While we all appreciated your intention, it would be best if you stayed in your room. We need to keep order here, Kate".

"How can you let her in to visiting hours? My Twin replied, infuriated and suddenly exhausted.

"It's not up to us," she said and closed the door. My Twin lay motionless, staring at the ceiling.

My Twin stayed in her room for the rest of the day and night. They brought her lunch and dinner, but she didn't eat.

The good news came with the next evening moon. The court had been in contact with Sofia, the Debutante Southern Belle in New York, and she had sent the proper paperwork to have my Twin released when the judge was back in chambers. The family that called it in would be arriving to take her home with them first thing Tuesday morning. Archangel Uriel hovered over Kate while Kate scribbled on a piece of paper she pulled from her pocket.

Plato said, "I lived my life," while I cried for mine. I listened to the lullabies, but I still got left behind. I hear the violins, and I still cry my tears. I dance to my own symphony, but I still wear my fears. A cloth of sadness covers me, and my lonely heart cries. All the songs say so as I wave my last good-byes.

—Age 16½

Chapter 6
I'm Not Cinderella

Tuesday came and went, and Kate was now living with the redheaded woman, Rachelle, and her five sons in the desert of Las Vegas. The eleventh grade was underway when one of the sons, Dillon, would profess his love for her and give her someone to hold onto. He reminded her how to smoke pot. He was also an A student, a genius like Paige. He helped her study in the hope that she would become the A student that he was, and he even took her to interviews so that she could get her first job.

The day came when she had to learn to share him with his first car. Around the same time, the then-sober Rachelle brought her new fiancé and his son home for dinner. Within three months, she was married, and they all moved into a five-bedroom estate owned by the new husband. Things were looking up.

Kate got a job as a receptionist in a telemarketing company. Dillon would take her to school at 7:00 a.m. and pick her up at 1:30 p.m. to get her to the job by 2:00 p.m. She finished work at 8:00 p.m. and would get home in time to do homework and get some sleep. She would crawl into bed with Dillon, and they would talk and cry and hug and love each other as best as their pasts would allow.

Dillon told her about his drunken father, who would beat

him, and the drunken Rachelle, who wouldn't defend him or his brothers. He shared with her all the horrible stories that made him who he was, and Kate was thankful for someone to relate to. Again.

Sometime when Dillon and Kate were away at school or work, Rachelle took up drinking again. Kate could see why she had given it up in the first place, and the boys were all terribly reminded. The tension in the house took on a life of its own, and everyone was walking around on eggshells. Kate was thankful for not having to ever be at the dinner table with the eight of them, but she would have at least liked some dinner.

After seven months of my Twin and Dillon being together, Rachelle found out and blew a drunken gasket. Her way of coping with how much her precious Dillon and Kate loved each other was to treat Kate like a live-in maid. She was to vacuum the house and take out the trash and water the plants. Sometimes Dillon would help her, but sometimes he had to study for a test, which was more important. When she got home from her day, the dishes from dinner were waiting for her in the kitchen. With suds to her elbows and tears sliding down her face into the dirty dishwater, Kate robotically performed her chores. Staring out the window, she listened to her internal dialogue asking the same old questions.

Kate and Dillon started fighting all the time, and they realized they were too young to be together and deal with the always-drunk Rachelle while trying to finish high school. Dillon didn't want them to break up, but Kate assured him they had to. It was for the best. Kate didn't tell him that she had found someone who could save her from the hell she was living in. She didn't want to further break his heart or her own, but her boss was showing a liking to her, and she liked it.

Archangel Uriel was quick to be at my side. "This poor girl. Whatever this karma was of that Lord Hadrian, it must have been really bad. Why do I feel like we are about to embark on another tragic event for Kate?" I asked.

"I know Kate. I feel it, too," was all he said as he quickly started writing in another of many scrolls.

> Masquerade hearts don't keep from getting broken, and what we dwell on becomes our identity. I don't want to wear it anymore. A wink. A smile. A laugh. Emotions on my sleeve, and I feel I'm torn in half. Is there a happily ever after in the land of effervescent rainbows? Paintings find me peaceful, and I welcome the quiet. I try to gather my thoughts but am easily distracted. The hazel eyes of a wolf intrigue me. Come for me. The statue of a woman who stands on her own. Flowers on a table, and I feel so far from home. Nothing left to be forgotten, and you're looking through Oscar Wilde's memory. I'm trying to listen to my life that has so much to say. Can you unravel me? Hunger finds me vulnerable, and I feel shy. It calls out to me. I'm not sure why. Dance with me barefoot and kiss my mouth. Waterfall lyrics reveal me. What's this? A coin in a wishing well, one I must have missed. Once upon a time of fascination. A glimpse. A tingle. A Breath. No more disguise. Just a girl with kaleidoscope eyes.
>
> —Age 17

A new guy started at the telemarketing office not long after Kate had settled in nicely to her new job. Logan had moved to Las Vegas from the East Coast; he was cute, funny, and he looked at Kate with a level of fondness that was a little too much for my taste, considering he was ten years her senior. Logan was quick to move offices so he could talk to her from his desk. He was a hard worker, albeit a bit of a workaholic; I'll give him that. He would buy takeout for them, and they would eat together. They did make a great team, and I noticed Kate looked forward to going to work each day. They worked hard to make him a lot of money, and in return, he got her a raise and had her promoted to his assistant. Brownie points for him.

My Twin and Logan seemed to have a bottomless connection. Maybe it was because they were both from the East Coast, or maybe it was because they both loved takeout. My Twin found him to be easy to talk to, and he seemed to be everything she thought she would never find in a man.

It all seemed like a fairy tale to Kate. Though she knew the true circumstances of her relationship, she couldn't help but feel as if it were a scene out of a romance novel, where a beautiful princess locks eyes with a prince across the ballroom. Of course, their ballroom was an office with a few rows of cubicles and quietly humming computers.

Each day, she looked forward to seeing him. She took extra time getting ready, because knowing that he would see her made her want to impress him. Though she didn't think he would ever ask her to dress a certain way or do her hair to please him, she could tell that he really appreciated her appearance, and she felt justified in making the extra effort.

They stole glances at one another across the office. He would make up silly reasons to come talk to her. He would ask her questions he knew the answer to or ask if she needed anything from the supply closet. She would ask him if he needed any coffee when she walked by his desk, just to get the opportunity to speak with him. They made sure to sit by one another in staff meetings, and he would save a seat for her on the bench outside when they took their breaks.

When they left work, they would walk to the parking lot together. I could feel when Kate cherished the moments when the backs of their hands would brush against each other as they walked. The touch was electric. The simple grazing of skin sent shock waves to her core. She couldn't pinpoint the exact moment she fell in love with him, but she knew that those few stolen touches, innocent and simple, were what solidified her love for him. And perhaps they were what made her choose to open up to him.

Working late one night, eating Chinese takeout, Kate told him what had happened to her in California. She told him how she was taken away from her father, and she told him about the family that she was living with and how they were treating her. He placed his hands on her face, looked into her eyes, and said, "My sweet little Cinderella, no one will ever hurt you again." And with that he kissed her. It was the most sensual thing that had ever happened to her. That night he drove her home, parked in front of the house, and he kissed her again. Dillon, who was still in love with her, saw them from the window and moved out of the house the next day. Kate moved out the following day and into Logan's apartment.

Though Kate had moved several times throughout her life, this was one of the few times she was genuinely excited to do so. There was no one forcing her. She wasn't being trundled from one guardian to another. This time it was her choice. She was finally becoming the person she always wanted to be and living up to her potential. And she was in love with a man who understood that.

When she moved into his apartment, she was overjoyed to see that he had made space for her. There was a whole rack in the closet, though she didn't have nearly half enough outfits to fill it. He put an extra shelf in the living room for her to put some of her things on, like records, books, and photos. Her whole life, she had lived in places that belonged to other people.

Like most new couples, they shared some awkward moments. But there was never anything so awful that they couldn't get over it. Kate truly cherished the moments when she and Logan spent time in the kitchen, sautéing vegetables and cooking pasta, splitting a pot of coffee, or even just chatting over the Sunday paper.

I wasn't happy that Kate stopped going to high school, and I was worried that there were holes in her memory—large chunks of missing pieces that I tried to hold onto for her but couldn't. It's not how this worked. Archangel Zadkiel must have felt my concern, because he appeared at my side with his precious violet flames of light around him. They always brought comfort. "I did some intel on this," he said. "And it would seem that the tragic events in her life are causing the memory lapses, and I don't see her getting them back. It's like her mind is so strong she is able to block out that which she thinks doesn't serve her. The scrolls indicate that Kate will come to study the mind and be so intrigued by the concepts that she will one day hopefully find congruency between her mind, her body, and her spirit. It seems that the conscious mind has limited access to memories, and the subconscious mind has virtually infinite memory. It is human recall that is culpable."

Though they stayed busy at work, they made time for each other when they got home each night. If they were too exhausted to cook and chat about the day, they would simply order a pizza and sit on the couch together to watch the evening news or sitcom reruns. She always felt safe in his arms and had no trouble falling asleep, safe in the warmth of his embrace as the glow of the television illuminated their living room. She was so happy and peaceful.

They had been together for almost a year when his talkative but nice mother came to visit. She was excited about meeting her son's new girlfriend, the first one he had ever "brought home" to meet her. They were on his boat on Lake Mead, enjoying the pleasant afternoon sun, when Carissa, his mother realized Kate would be a high school senior if she were actually going to school, which would make her only seventeen years old.

At that point, Carissa looked toward her son and said, "Logan, this is scandalous. Your father is rolling over in his grave right now." She couldn't see how her son—her pride and joy—could engage in a relationship with a minor. How did he not see the danger?

Carissa wasn't the sort of person to engage in confrontation. She calmly asked Logan to return to the dock immediately. Back at the dock, she scrambled off the boat and headed for the car without waiting for her son to tie up the boat.

Kate's stomach knotted up, compounding her anxiety and nerves. She knew his mother's approval was important to the man she loved, and she couldn't imagine what their relationship would be like now that Carissa officially disapproved.

She helped him grab the ice chest from the boat and looked at him. "Are you okay?" she asked.

He didn't look at her. His voice was quiet and without energy. "We'll talk later. Let's get back to the apartment."

My Twin could feel a coldness wash over her. He had never brushed her off like that. It was a bad sign.

They drove back to the apartment in silence. Carissa stared out the window and pretended that neither of them where there.

The rest of the day was a marathon of soft-spoken debate. Kate didn't know how to feel about this. *Why weren't we yelling and name calling like my family did?* she thought as she sat on the bed with the door closed. She pulled her knees up tight to her chin. She didn't even take off her swimsuit from the boat trip. Instead, she hunkered down in the bedroom and closed the blinds. She couldn't hear everything that was said, but she knew it wasn't good. Carissa cut the trip short and boarded a plane for the East Coast. Kate and Logan continued working and living together, and everyone at the telemarketing company made a lot of money. There were six sales guys, each with their own assistant. They worked hard by day and partied hard by night.

Most nights, they would go out to dinner after work as a group. My Twin loved it because they had enough money to do it, and since she was still underage, dinner was one of the few things she could do with the rest of her coworkers. She really enjoyed their company and felt like the nights they spent dining at fancy Italian restaurants were some of the best nights of her life.

But some nights, the men would go out together, leaving their assistants to fend for themselves. At first, it only happened a couple of nights a month. But then, it became a weekly and soon a daily thing. Kate could feel a distance growing between her and Logan.

The minute I saw Logan doing cocaine with his friends, I called for the Archangels *stat*. It was Archangel Michael who answered my call. "There's a pattern emerging that we can't do anything about. Remember what Howard Wills told us about ancestral patterns and habits. It is human nature to attract to them all that they know. Kate grew up in a household with a father who fits the characteristics of the life she was attracting. It would take her time and more dark experiences before she would come to this realization on her own through the work we would lead her to do. In the meantime, she was blinded to the patterns. Most people go through their whole lives and never wake up to these realizations, but we will help Kate open her eyes and her heart." Defeated again, I said, "We're just going to watch and

hope she actually makes it to the day you can show yourselves."
His reply was sobering.

"It would seem so," he said.

Logan became paranoid, protective, and overbearing toward
my Twin. No surprise there. We had seen this before, but Kate—
as Archangel Michael told me—was blind to it.

One morning, Logan woke up and was extremely rude to
Kate. He barely spoke a word to her for three days. He just drank
and went out with his friends after work. On one of her many
attempts to confront him, he admitted, "I'm sorry. I was wrong
to treat you this way. I had a dream that you were in the arms
of another man, and it was so real it made me so mad. I didn't
know what to do with the feelings I was having." Afterwards, they
laughed about the dream. But something had changed about him.

Maybe it was because Kate was so young that she couldn't
figure it out immediately. But on the nights he would go out and
do cocaine, he wouldn't let her go out. Instead, he made sure she
was at home and locked up tight, even if a friend of hers invited
her to a girls' night out. He just didn't trust her anymore. Maybe
it was because Carissa didn't approve of Kate or because the drugs
were making him paranoid. Whatever it was, it meant that my
Twin was slowly becoming a prisoner again. History really does
have a way of repeating itself.

She spent many nights in the apartment, curled up on the
couch and waiting for him to come home. She would fall asleep
watching TV and worrying about his safety. She still trusted him,
even though he didn't always deserve it, but she couldn't help but
feel like something awful was going on.

He eventually began to bring the drugs home, so she knew
for certain what he was up to. A few of their coworkers came over,
and they planned to go out to an all-ages dance club where my
Twin could also get in.

Kate and some of the women were getting ready in the bathroom while Logan and the men sat in the living room, drinking beer. Kate was excited. She wasn't always able to go out with the group, but tonight they'd made allowances for her young age, and she was excited to go out with them.

"I love your hair," one of the assistants said to my Twin. "It always looks great, but when you do it up to go out, it looks amazing."

My Twin blushed.

"Thanks. I just like to have it up if I'm going to dance, since I'll probably get hot."

"No, really, you're really pretty. It's no wonder the boss likes you so much," she said with a wink.

My Twin couldn't help but feel special. She couldn't wait to have fun with the man she loved, and it didn't hurt that someone was telling her how great she looked.

As the girls finished putting on their makeup, they stepped into the living room. Some of the men whistled jokingly, and others put arms around their significant others. But Logan didn't say or do anything. Instead, he gave Kate a look that made her blood run cold. He glared at her until she stared uncomfortably down at the floor.

At the time, she didn't know it was the drugs; she thought it was something she was or wasn't doing. But they would all be partying at the house, and when it was time to go out, Logan would say my Twin couldn't go and she wouldn't see him again until morning. He started verbally abusing her and treated her as if she was nothing. He called her stupid and told her that nothing she ever said was intelligent. And she believed everything he said. If only she could have seen through his insecurities and ignorance. But she was too young and naïve and in love to know what was really happening. He was the first solid thing to happen to her, but her intelligence, her youth, and her independence threatened him. If only she knew enough not to let him wash it all down the drain. I watched as Kate cried herself to sleep on the couch, a regular occurrence I wasn't keen on at all. The dream came so quickly I could barely catch my breath.

The castle and its surrounding grounds sparkled with life and the sun was so bright I had to shield my eyes from its compelling smile. The sounds of pretty bagpipes reached my ears from the far side of the back lawn. The shrubbery was well manicured with shapes of deer, horses, and dragons majestic as if they were the guardians of the land. I could see that beyond the immediate lawn was a maze with over three miles of paths on three acres. It was a traditional hedge in the shape of a labyrinth, with thousands of colorful plants, including hibiscus, roses, and sunflowers strategically placed throughout. My attention was pulled back to the main lawn, where hundreds of people sat in simple white chairs in front of a gorgeous vine-covered pergola. A waterfall was soothing as its backdrop. It was a grand court with a cheerful crowd and anticipation in the air. Almost immediately, the wedding march of a grand piano joined the bagpipes, accompanied by the lovely sound of flutes. A beautiful woman appeared at the opening of the aisle wearing the most elegant gown of white silk covered in pearls and lace. Her hair glistened with a crown of jewels and a pearl- embellished veil obscured her face. A hush fell over the crowd as this lovely princess walked arm-in-arm with her father, a King from another land. As she approached the podium and Lord Hadrian, we all watched as the veil was lifted and her father kissed her cheek. He put her hand in the hand of Lord Hadrian as they both smiled and faced the high priest.

"Lord Hadrian. Do you take this—" Was quickly drowned out by the realization that there were dragons among them, and Kate woke up with a start, gasping for air. I watched her shake her head, look around at the empty living room, drag herself into the empty bedroom, and crawl into bed.

With another dream forgotten and life setting in like a bad rerun, I watched the relationship sap my Twin's energy. It took everything she had to try to make him happy when he would fly into his paranoid rages. And she still didn't understand that it wasn't her fault and that no matter what she did, it wouldn't matter because the problem was his.

One morning when Logan was completely wasted, they got into a big fight. He had been out all night long and had come home around 10:00 a.m. He found Kate sleeping on the couch in the same place she had fallen asleep while waiting for him. Instead of leaving her alone, he pulled the blanket off her and began to yell.

"Get up! You're so lazy. This house is a mess. When I come home, I want to come home to a clean house!"

It took Kate a moment to wake up enough to realize that it wasn't a dream she was having and that her boyfriend, the man she loved, was in a strange mood. She tried to stand, but he pushed her back down.

"I'm so sick of this!" he yelled. He stormed into the kitchen and began throwing dishes.

She chased after him to stop him, but as she tried to grab a bowl from his hands, he knocked her down. She stood up and raced into the bedroom, trying to get away from this unknown man. He chased after her, screaming maniacally. He threw her down on the bed and yelled at her, blaming her for a recent drop in sales that was due to his drug use and had nothing to do with her. He swung his fists wildly, almost hitting her several times. He turned to leave the room.

My Twin stood up and rushed to the door, hoping and praying

she could say something to make him change. She thought maybe if she tried hard enough, she could brighten his mood.

But before she could reach him, he stormed out of the room and slammed the door.

My Twin was overcome with emotion. Everything welled up inside of her—fear, anger, confusion, and disappointment—overwhelming her and mixing with a general feeling of illness. Her face became hot while her hands became clammy. The room seemed to swirl around her. She couldn't tell if the floor was moving or if she was the only one feeling it. She wondered to herself if she was in some sort of earthquake, which would explain the feeling of movement. But why did it feel as if her head were under water? Her breath came in short gasps, and she fell to the ground. She had fainted.

In her unconscious state, she dreamed, and as I followed the path of her voice, I found her sitting with Archangel Zadkiel, talking.

"I am trying very hard to stay optimistic on my journey. This test of nature versus nurture that I somehow signed myself up for is like an amusement park ride. I get dizzy. I find myself one minute ecstatic at the prospect of what lies ahead, but all of these obstacles set me off, and I question my own beliefs and purpose. Sometimes I let people and circumstances get the best of me. Sometimes I let *myself* get the best of me! And if I'm not careful, my frustration can cover me in a veil of contention. I get affected; it's true. I expect people to have integrity—to be honest, loyal, and caring. But I expect too much. I expect too much of people and of myself. If I could be granted one wish in life, my wish would be that everyone achieves a state of empathy. But I think I'm going off on a tangent. Why do I keep finding myself in these circumstances? What did I do to deserve this? Look at what's happened to me. I'm falling into an abyss that I may never get out of. Is it my turn to die now?"

It was Archangel Zadkiels' turn to speak,

"As a 'people,' you are far from flawless. And that's okay. Your flaws give you character. It's your flaws that teach you how to be better but allow you to be human. Growing up knowing that whatever you did would never be good enough for the Genius Mother who birthed you was draining, to say the least. Of all the things you need to let go of in life, this has been one of your biggest challenges. But you know this path you're on is far from over. Let yourself off the proverbial hook you've been hanging from. This marks the end of this part of the story. You will get up from this, and you will leave this environment immediately. You will not take anything with you. You are to call your mother and tell her what is happening to you, and she will send for you. You will fly home to her at once. Now wake up!"

The Boss never even knew she had fainted, and she wouldn't remember the message Archangel Zadkiel tried to implant in her mind.

She didn't know how long he'd been gone when she finally came to. Her face was tear-stained and she felt nauseated. She didn't stand up for a few minutes; afraid she would take another fall. Instead, she sat very still; breathing deeply and wishing the headache would go away. She had a few bruises from the fall, but other than that, she felt okay. But little did she know she would carry the emotional scars from Logan's outburst for a long time.

She tried to write it off, but it didn't make sense. She had never fainted before, and she figured it was just a fluke. She also couldn't help but think there was a message she was supposed to remember. Shaking her head and getting up from the floor, she reasoned that it must have been brought on by the intensity of her emotions. It was probably nothing to worry about, so she pushed it out of her head. She went about her day and waited for Logan to come home and apologize.

She tried not to think about the fight they'd had. She decided she would focus on the future instead of the past. She began to clean the apartment, scouring it from top to bottom. Cleaning had always made her feel better, like she was cleansing her whole environment and could start fresh. She swept up the broken plates. She really loved the pattern on the china, but knew there was no use crying over its loss. It was best to just sweep up the fragments and throw them away. Besides, she could always buy new plates.

Though bending down to sweep the little shards into the dustpan made my Twin feel a little dizzy, she kept working diligently, trying to get the apartment into tip-top shape. She polished the wood on the cabinets in the kitchen, washed all the dishes, cleaned out the fridge, and mopped the floor. She dusted and vacuumed the living room; she fluffed the cushions on the couch and threw away the old magazines on the coffee table.

She began to feel exhausted. She lay down on the couch for a moment and checked the clock. It was getting late in the day, and she still hadn't heard from him. Her head was starting to ache, but she didn't want to stop cleaning. She had made so much progress. And with Logan partying in the apartment with his friends a few nights a week, it was getting hard to stay on top of the mess.

She stood up and felt a wave of nausea hit her hard. Standing still for a moment, she let it pass. She told herself that it was most likely just from the stress of the past few days. Slowly, she made her way down the hall and into the bathroom.

She started with the sink and then cleaned the toilet. The smell of bleach wafted through the air. It wasn't strong, but it was enough to be noticed. She stepped into the bathtub and began to scrub the tile walls. As she made vigorous circles on the walls with her scrub brush, she began to feel lightheaded. But she didn't want to stop; she was almost done.

Little flecks of light filled her vision, and her sight began to dim around the edges. She remembered seeing the white foam of the cleaner slowly slide down the wall before everything went black, and then she remembered nothing.

She had fainted again. This time when she opened her eyes she was on the cold porcelain floor of the shower, and she was surrounded with blood, just as she remembered the Genius Mother lying in a blanket of her own blood.

She didn't know whom to call. Logan was nowhere to be found, and with his temper lately, he would probably think she was making it all up. She didn't want to make him mad. She also knew she couldn't call anyone from the telemarketing company because it would make him look like a bad boyfriend if he wasn't available to take her to the doctor. She couldn't call Alex or his wife, because she had worked so hard to get away from them.

She called Mia, who was also living in Las Vegas now, and told her to come and get her. It had been a long time since they had spoken to one another, but she knew her sister would help her.

The sisters went to the emergency room, and the attending doctor couldn't believe Kate was still standing. She was ninety-five pounds, had miscarried an ectopic pregnancy, and was bleeding internally. The doctor said to Mia, "Wow, Someone from above must be looking out for your sister, because you got her here just in time. One more hour and she'd be gone."

There was no way the doctor could know how much we had been looking out for her.

Over the next six months, Mia got married and moved away, and Kate stayed in the abusive relationship because she felt she had nowhere else to go. She was still working at the office with him, and they were all business-as-usual in front of everyone else.

After work, most nights, he went to hang out with his friends, and she would stay awake at night, wondering if he was going to come back or if he had found someone new. He was so wasted all the time that he didn't even notice her spark was all but gone. In a rare moment of clarity, my Twin knew that if she didn't get out of there soon, she would die. She was barely eighteen.

Her body moved restlessly as she slept, but the undeniable voice and familiar demand of Archangel Zadkiel rang through my ears as he tried again to reach her. "This marks the end of this part of the story. You will get up from this, and you will leave this environment immediately. You will not take anything with you. You are to call the Genius Mother and tell her what is happening to you, and she will send for you. You will fly home to her at once. Now wake up!"

The next day, when the Boss was at work, Kate had a strong compulsion to call her mother, who was now living in Brooklyn on her own. She told Paige everything, crying into the phone and asking her to please tell her what to do. Two hours later, she was boarding a flight; by the time Logan got home from his day, my Twin was long gone. With Kate safely tucked away into a seat in economy, Archangel Zadkiel was scribbling in his scroll while Kate was writing in her now almost-full notebook with the occasional tear quietly joining her words on the page.

> Warm weather on the water and the rippling reminds me of moving forward. With a strong sense of propriety, I've decided my handbook must be missing pages. Missteps and mayhem keep the humor alive, and it's ironic that I have a sense of comedic timing at all. One step forward and two steps back, and thank God for second chances. While not being privy to all of the instructions

may be cause for alarm, our common sense should be able to fill in the blanks. Life is a like a game of ad-libs. Venture to follow the culprit of necessary struggles, and herein lies the rub. It's in the struggles that we can become friends with our sunny disposition. If everything were easy, who would that make us? When putting ourselves together, we need to have some faith. We need to know when to use a little WD-40 to loosen our grasp and when we should take out the wrench to help rein it all in. Assimilate all there is to be thankful for, and widen your reach. When you find yourself somewhere you don't fit, laugh it off. Embrace the differences of every piece of the puzzle. Accept that what you bring to the table might just round out the edges. Don't be homogenized in someone else's Scrabble game. Know who you are and spell it out loud and clear. Even if you're missing a letter, don't let it keep you from being you. As long as you are learning and thinking outside the box, you are automatically adjusting according to size. Don't be afraid that a little assembly is required. Keep rolling the dice and see where it takes you. There are usually a few bolts left over anyway, right? Hold on to those leftover bits like they're Monopoly pieces. Let them be your get-out-of-jail-free card.

—Age 18

Chapter 7
Coast to Coast

Kate arrived in New York on a balmy spring day, but she couldn't wait to get in bed and go to sleep. Her trying to make sense of her life and the unsuccessful replaying of its events was exhausting. Now here she was with the Genius Mother, who was older and who no longer seemed to judge her. That was new.

They were both quiet on the bus ride back to Paige's new apartment, which was fine for both of them. Without unpacking her one small bag of belongings, Kate sat on the couch, taking in her surroundings, and soon fell fast asleep.

She dreamt of a key that carried a message. In her hand, it felt like cold nickel-plated brass but was mixed with old-world charm. It left her wondering if she had missed something. Where had she left those memories again? Holding the key up to the light caused the reflected light to cast a shadow on the wall in the shape of a heart. An emblem of love? She counted the teeth, thinking the dips and valleys were symbolic in some way, and she couldn't help but wonder if they were the perfect match to a keyhole somewhere she didn't have directions to. The key wasn't quite a skeleton key, and she knew instinctively that it wouldn't open just any door. Maybe it was the key to the gateway to the future. Perhaps it would be her way out.

I could see someone in the distance, and my Twin must have seen them too as she headed toward the distant figure, calling out, "Archangel Gabriel is that you? Have I gone from Neverland to Wonderland, where there's no more living between lives? How many lifetimes do I have to live before I get it right, anyway? Did it all squeeze into one? I hope I don't end up in some house of mirrors and have to face them all. What would I say? Gabriel? Can you hear me?"

Another part of myself was trying to cross the barriers at the speed of light with her. *Now, this is an interesting dream,* I thought.

"If it's one at a time and comes with answers, I can handle that. I need answers." But her words were met with silence. Time passed, and then Archangel Gabriel turned slowly and said, "Some journeys must be traveled alone. What kind of doorway are you looking for?"

My Twin shook her head at him, but still she took the step into the confidence of a resource cloak. As she stepped forward, I was able to step closer to crossing through the threshold of where yesterday meets tomorrow. There, I found my Twin, older and looking quizzically in a mirror. Inside the mirror were palm trees and in the distance, an ocean.

She was lost in thought, and I hoped an answer would reveal itself, but the dream continued on.

I could hear my Twin whispering and knew instinctively this was Archangel Uriels' doing. "To keep my life from being someone else's metaphor, I embrace my courage," she said quietly. "The key seems to hold the same principles as a compass. Who am I not to follow? It seems to be taking me on a walkabout. A journey where there is no past and no future. The silence is like music played on another kind of keys, and it makes me smile. I'm not in a hurry, and I don't feel lost. I'm alone but I'm not lonely. I feel a love that seems to be emanating from my core or from above or all around me. Oh, that's what this feels like. How compassionate. Is this what I've been looking for outside myself? Somehow, I've lost my way. I got tangled in the fabrication of misinformation instilled in me in childhood. Blinded by transference and wounded by disregard, I suddenly feel this strong sense that I have a calling."

My attention was drawn immediately to Archangel Gabriel, smiling as the key in my Twin's hand glistened and glowed with anticipation. In my peripheral vision, I was distracted by a sunbeam of light, impressively bright and welcoming. It radiated from Archangel Raphael and blasted through the keyhole of a simple, yet familiar doorway.

Instinctively, my Twin reached her hand toward the door, and the key fit perfectly. As she slowly opened the door and peeked behind it, I thought she was going to see her team of archangels working away in their respective workspaces, but instead, her reflection greeted her in another large framed mirror.

That feeling came over her again, and key in hand, she attempted to walk into the mirror. But she was woken up by her Genius Mother's music on the stereo, and she was back at the new apartment in Brooklyn.

Looking around the apartment, I knew time had passed. Two years had gone by, and my Twin was back in the California sand where she would meet a true Street Kid of her own.

She was living in a small house in Venice that she shared with Gentry, the son of the Guardians she used to live with.

Archangel Michael appeared by my side, "It is hard to watch Kate walk blindly through this life unaware. But this life will lead her to the answers that will bring change to the world on a large scale. Her past will lead her on a quest to share her insights with the world. She's not the only one. So many people are living in transference and repeating their ancestral patterns because— believe it or not—their current actions are congruent with their subconscious belief systems instilled in them in childhood. But we know she will figure this out and we will help her. So stay patient as we comfort her from afar as she goes down yet again another one of her rabbit holes".

I watched as the months passed and Kate made new friends now living in Venice, California. She was waiting tables at a local restaurant, a favor Gentry had pulled with the manager. She was going through the motions of tending to her customers when I felt a familiar feeling wash over her. When I looked to see what she was looking at, I knew instinctively it was going to happen again. She had a crush on him the moment he walked through the door, and there was nothing the Archangels or I could do to stop it. He stayed at the bar for all of her shift as they flirted with each other every time Kate went for drinks to serve. Later that night she and her best friend joined him for margaritas and the free concert at the Pier. They listened to him tell his stories. When he got up to use the bathroom, my Twin looked at her friend and said, "He's mine, so didn't even think about flirting with him."

As he rejoined them at the table and continued his stories, the red flags were everywhere. But she didn't want to see them. "Archangel Michael, do you hear her? She's trying to rationalize it. I think her subconscious must be picking up on all the similarities that he has with the original Street Kid and the Genius Mother, but she's suppressing the warnings as fast as they come."

"Yes. I know. She is submerging herself again into the negative love syndrome she grew up in," he said matter-of-factly. As I watched, I knew there was no turning back now. I watched for months as they slept in the same bed but didn't sleep together. They shared stories of their pasts. They bonded over the pain, the sorrow, and the loss they had in common. They were philosophical and engaging. It was all so beyond hopelessly familiar.

Then one day in a fight with him on the phone, she called

him a joke and hung up on him. She couldn't say why she did it, though it was probably something she should've said to many men in her life. It just came out that day, and he happened to hear it.

A half hour later, he barged through the door and pulled my Twin out of the shower by her hair. At some time during the ensuing screaming match, when she thought for sure he was going to hit her, he leaned toward her and spat in her face. She was frozen and mortified.

My Twin didn't know how to react. She had no idea how disrespectful this Drake could be, and she wasn't happy to find out. She felt pure emotion take over. It must have triggered a rape flashback, because she came out of a hiding place and couldn't remember going into it. Three hours after the attack, she emerged from hiding in the closet to find him crying in the living room. He apologized profusely and said nothing like this would ever happen again. He said that he had fallen in love with her, and he was afraid.

She asked him to leave, telling him that she had to think, but what she really wanted was to go to sleep. That's where she had come to learn where the messages were hiding. She lay down on her bed, her tear-stained face on the pillow, settling into the familiarity of it all. *Life sure does have a funny way of repeating itself over and over,* I thought. I couldn't stop myself from wondering, *where will this take her?*

I could hear the voice of Archangel Uriel and knew Kate was sleeping. Her dream was different from the other ones; I just couldn't figure out what it meant. It was a different version of Kate. She looked like she was in the 1800s, and she sat at an antique writing desk wearing a long beige nightdress that stroked the dusty hardwood floors whenever she moved slightly in her seat. Her hair was tied back by a rope, brown waves cascading around her face and shoulders. Her face was pale and fragile, her eyes as green as emeralds. She had ivory parchment in front of her and a quill in her hand. I could see Archangel Uriel dictating aloud as he scribbled in his scroll. I wondered if she could hear him. She filled the page, the occasional tear falling freely and smearing some of the ink.

It is said that we do the same things again and again, even if it hurts us or depletes us, because it is all we know. So the payoff (even if painful) is still a payoff. I don't know much, but this sounds to me like the definition of insanity. Doing the same thing over and over and expecting a different outcome. The outcomes of our lives are born from our choices. The choices that we make about how we want things to go. We choose to give up or to persevere. We choose which path we will walk, and we choose which songs we will dance to. We choose whom we love, but sometimes love chooses for us. We are constantly making choices, whether we realize it or not. Consciously and subconsciously, in every moment, we are making a choice about something, about everything.

But sometimes our choices were made for us long ago in another time and place, and we have to succumb to the lessons. This is karma. And I will come …

Kate jerked awake to the sound of her ringing phone. The voice on the other end told her that she had booked the lead part in an independent film and that principal photography was starting right away. In her excitement about the news, she forgot all about the dream and the messages the archangels were trying to tell her. But I didn't. I would ponder the words for days while

I stood on the sidelines and watched my Twin yet again fall down the proverbial rabbit hole.

She had to go to sleep early on work nights and was constantly working on her material. She was so busy that she hadn't even noticed that her roommate (and then best friend) was hanging out with Drake all the time.

Kate got home from work one day and had the most horrible feeling. Her intuition screamed that her roommate and Drake had slept together, but she couldn't prove it. She was reliving verbatim the accusations in her parents' troubled past. She was in transference and she couldn't get out. Drake was also trapped, because somehow in all the arguing, they had thought it would be a good idea to move in together.

I wanted to cover my eyes.

Shortly after the move, my Twin booked another job and would be leaving to go on the road in a month's time. Getting this job and traveling should have been the most exciting time of her life, but Drake made it one of the most miserable. The pattern was repeating, but Kate didn't know how to get out of it.

For five years we watched Kate in a relationship that would spiritually break her and emotionally cripple her. She was forever chasing the moments when they showed each other their versions of love. He was great at surprising her with gifts and candlelight dinners and picnics. She was like an addict chasing a high. But those moments were few and far between, and there was no happy medium. They were both engaged in some horrible pattern—a version of negative love syndrome—and they could not see through the darkness. His misplaced anger was met by her thinking that this was all she deserved.

Continuing to lie to herself, Kate pretended not to see the lipstick on his collar or notice the women who would call for him. She knew that if she went through the motions at home, she could go to work and not have to think about it. When she was with him, she was trapped on an emotional rollercoaster. She would smile at him and kiss him on the cheek when she came home, but she felt something was wrong. If he truly loved her, he would have noticed that her heart wasn't in the relationship and that she made excuses not to be in the same room with him. Of course, that was on the good days. On the bad days, my Twin was reduced to tears, crying her heart out at the coldness. But she didn't know there was anything else out there for her. And he had said he loved her, so she believed that this relationship was love.

One night, as she tossed and turned in bed, Archangel Raphael brought Kate to the healing space of the mountain in her dream. The tree of life stood glowing and omnipresent. The slight breeze caused the leaves to sing, and the grass reached up to join in the choir. The archangels were in different states of meditation, and colored beams of light matched the aura of the tree. It was as if the different colors of the chakras were being represented, and it was breathtaking to watch.

Kneeling before the tree with tears in her eyes, Kate spoke quietly and breathily as the droplets of her life streamed from her eyes. "As much as I hate to admit it, I do have feelings. I am not the New York tough girl with a shell of knight's armor that I show the world. I am susceptible to harm, I get sad, and my feelings get hurt. Sometimes I am lost, I lack direction, and I go in circles. It's as if I have become my mother and I'm living her life over and over. I am vulnerable. *Eek!* The V word! To me the V word was the equivalent to most people's L word. But here goes. I am trying something new. These are my humble admissions."

At first I thought it was one of the archangels who spoke, but it was Howard Wills and he seemed to be deeply connected to the Tree of Life standing majestically in front of us.

As Kate listened, Howard spoke. "Know you attract that

which you know. It is human nature that you will create situations that prove you right. Without awareness, you will keep repeating your patterns, and you won't be able to get off the hamster wheel. What you see in childhood is what you learn to cope with in adulthood. These confessions do not cast blame. They come out very one-sided, but that's good! This is your journey. The scrolls have deemed it so. No one sees the list. And you certainly shouldn't have to defend it, not to anyone and most certainly not to yourself. You react to things based on your own knowledge, feelings, and upbringing. This comes from the ancestors of your lineage. The work you will do for yourself will be open, raw, and life changing. You are hurting, and you are confused. You don't understand your life's events, but you will. You were made in the eyes of greatness, to fulfill a destiny that is bigger than you. People who care about you don't hurt you on purpose. Chances are high that they are not aware of what they are doing. How can they be? They don't have your same perceptions or your same model of the world. You can't take it personally. If it hurts, feel the pain. Find the place of love in your heart, and forgive them and forgive yourself."

"Yes. It's actually been physically uncomfortable for me. When you spend your life protected behind your facade, it's scary as hell to step out from beyond the veil," my Twin replied.

I couldn't help but admire my Twin for how far she was coming, and I found myself silently praying that she would remember this when she woke.

My Twin became someone she never wanted to be, and when she and Drake broke up for the last time, there was no way for her to know the extent of the transference she was in. This relationship would make her question her past and give her the determination to change her future. Perhaps she would realize that she was more Paige's daughter than she cared to admit.

Howard continued. "It is almost time for you to wake," he said. Take this with you. Try to remember it."

> God, For Myself, My Spouse, All Our Family Members, All Our Relationships, All Our Ancestors And All Their Relationships Back Through All Time, Through All Of Our Lives God, Please Help Us All Forgive, Be Forgiven, And All Forgive Ourselves Completely And Totally, Now And Forever, Please God, Thank You God
>
> Lord, Fill Us All With Your Love And Give Us All Complete Peace Now And Forever, Please God, Thank You God
>
> God, We Thank You For Your Love, We Thank You For Your Blessings, We Thank You For The Gift Of Life And All The Many Gifts You Give Us Daily, Thank You God, Thank You God, Thank You God

Kate greeted the morning with what felt like hope. She grabbed her notebook and let herself be the conduit Archangel Uriel needed her to be, even if she wasn't aware of it yet.

> Wonderments of intrigue and a childish crush; music plays a symphony, and I just can't get enough. Strengths of the violin overtake the harp, all the while I think of you in a single moment's hush. The serenity of a rose-quartz crystal ball, sitting peacefully with just a smile, and the waterfall flows in tranquility. Dr. Seuss landings of a sacred space, and all is not forgotten. The world is filled with starlight, and I feel shy. A dog

barks in the distance, and a baby softly cries. Sleep doesn't find me now, so I am willful and awake. Sadness has no hold on me, but I wish to see your face. Black onyx to release memories of a past, just a girl with glistening eyes who knew it wouldn't last. How dost thou think of me if ever that you did? The crescent moon watches protectively, and I do so miss the snow. My eccentric Aquarius nature that I presume you already know—a lightning storm over the stillest of lakes, and I can still see the fireflies. Sparklers on my birthday cakes and memories of the pretty Genius Mother's smiles. Just a few distant thoughts of being happy as a child. Time heals all wounds and brings the ocean breeze. Now I sit quietly, getting sleepy, and I'm at peace. An unfinished painting stands by, beyond the candle's scent. Who shall play Brahms's lullaby so that sleep can find me easily? Will thy dreams come to me tonight and hold me, and will I find you there?

—Age 28

Chapter 8
Till Death Do Us Part

I have always prided myself on the strength of the shields my Twin had built around her. I mean, let's face it: after everything she'd been through, how could she not wear an "I can't hear you and nothing can hurt me now" suit of armor? I thought it was helping us keep her safe, until I realized she trusted no one and asked Archangel Michael if he thought the same.

"Archangel Michael, she seems to be closing herself off from the possibilities of change and growth in her spirit. I fear we weren't protecting her from the world. We were watching her shut it out. She can't possibly hear you guys like this, can she?" I pressed. It felt like denial but optimistic, and Kate had been going around in circles. They say that when the archangels speak, it sounds different to everyone. I could hear their words as they spoke to me, and it was always reassuring. But then again, I wasn't stuck on Earth like our Kate was.

Archangel Zadkiel appeared ready to issue some reassurances.

He smiled at me first and took my face in his hands. "When we speak to your twin, she doesn't always know it's us. We show her in her dreams, but as you know, she doesn't always remember them. When she does remember, she thinks they are only dreams. This will hopefully come to light soon."

"I know," I replied. "But then, what does she hear when you give her strength when she cries herself to sleep? What did she hear when she suffered the abuses? Or when she was lost and wandering? Did she hear the comforts you sent? Does she feel me?"

His smile broadened. "To your Twin, it starts out like a symphony. It's a musical composition the likes of which she has never heard before. It starts out quiet and slowly fills her soul, filling the holes in her heart. And then the words come in. She can't understand them at first because we do not speak in a human language. But the more she listens, the more she recognizes the meaning. It comes to her in poetry from Archangel Uriel; every time she exudes moments of power to move forward, Archangel Michael is feeding her strength of will. We are the conduits, and you are the link. The words are meant to let her know that she is not alone and that we are watching her. The music is meant to comfort her."

"That sounds beautiful," I said, realizing that I did know we were reaching her. How could we not be reaching her? I was watching her grow daily into a powerful and determined woman. But she still seemed so vulnerable and so alone, depleted and crushed by the memories of so many failed relationships and lack of family connections. I couldn't see past her frail and motionless body lying in the bed with only her sobs to comfort her.

Archangel Zadkiel continued. "Just as humans are all susceptible to pain, sorrow, and heartache, they are also capable of rising above it all, changing their story, and overcoming obstacles. Awareness is half the battle, and when they reach a fork in the road, the path they choose will set their course for life. They all grow up different. Humans all have regrets, demons, and apologies to make. They are born into someone else's story, and like many of them, your Twin was too young to make her decisions based on facts. She was born into circumstances beyond her control. Her life was chosen for her, and with that she would be blinded to the pain and suffering that would surround her. She saw what people wanted her to see. It kept her from knowing herself. But she is special. She has been chosen for a purpose, and she would have never been given anything she couldn't handle. She has a path to follow to clear up a debt that will eventually be revealed to her."

He continued. "Your Twin has strong determination. She has been growing stronger all her life. She knows she has had help. She knows there is something special and magical inside her, and she knows she is here for some bigger purpose. You have heard her say it: it is all unraveling. Her quest for knowledge and to fix her past and break free from the bonds she thinks have a hold on her will lead her to us. One day she will see us, and on that day she will know."

I found my Twin sad and wallowing over her failed relationship and missing the idea of the family that didn't exist for her. Listening to her try to make sense of it all was heart-wrenching. She was trying to make the puzzle pieces of the past fit with her decisions of today. She thought of them as mistakes; that message was undeniable. There were so many relentless questions streaming through her mind. If she thought clearly and wrote it all down, maybe she could make a timeline of her life that would match something, anything that would make sense of it all.

She wondered why she insisted on revisiting the darkness. Although she was caught in the web of thinking she deserved it, she was also convinced the darkness existed so she could appreciate what she would see when the sun came out from hiding. Sometimes she had to be reminded to let go, and sometimes the universe shifted just in time to teach her some new valuable lesson she didn't want to miss. Never one for taking the easy route, it was inevitable that in preparation for the change, she was humbled by this certain turn of events. How many times would she repeat the past? I could hear her telling herself that vulnerability was exposure, but what better time to fess up.

I took a long, hard look at what it all meant, and I get it now. She was admittedly human. She had fallen, but she had no visible scars or bruises. Through tears of frustration, she knew the minute it came full circle. She was completely hidden in the shadows where it was quiet and where the angelic sounds of wisdom could reach her. But then I heard her decide to let go. She gave herself over to what sense of truth she could find. She was using self-hypnosis guided imagery to rewrite her story.

My jaw must have dropped open when Archangel Gabriel appeared, laughing. "She is trying to find her way to us. This was always on the maps you saw Michael laboring over. It was just a matter of putting them together in a certain way to guide her down certain paths. It will still be a long and arduous journey— one that human life will try to get in the way of, but she will make it. She will come full circle, as life so needs to do."

"And just like with any eclipse, this too shall pass?" I couldn't help but ask meekly.

"The shadows will fall from her, and the light will show her who she is meant to be. Life happens, and as long as we guide her to learn and grow and evolve, the divine forces always help us stay the course," he said, and with that he was gone. She was writing in her notepad now. I knew Archangel Uriel was near but I was too busy trying to get a better look at what was being written.

> Have you ever peeked in the shadows to see what resides there?
> Now is as good a time as any.

> Lesson 1: When we play with fire, we will get burned.

Lesson 2: It's okay to say no if you're protecting yourself.

Lesson 3: Some friends don't want you to change.

Lesson 4: People make decisions based on their own selfish agenda.

Lesson 5: Most people are lost in their own darkness.

Lesson 6: If you ask for help, it comes.

Lesson 7: You are never alone. The divine force will never abandon you.

Lesson 8: From the hardest lessons come the most freedom.

Lesson 9: Brush yourself off and keep going.

Lesson 10: If you want something you've never got, you have to do something you've never done.

I think I know I am here for a reason and that whatever it is you have intended for me must be big. Perhaps in all this you have been helping me pay some kind of karmic debt, if there is such a thing. And if so, am I almost paid up now?

—Age 30

Maybe we were reaching her. My Twin spent most of life pursuing a relationship with Paige that she just wasn't capable of having. She didn't want anything to do with her. She was upfront about it. She had her issues and she knew it, but she wasn't wise enough rise above them. So Kate engaged. She reacted. She got sick and tired of Paige not caring about her, and at times she felt downright used and manipulated. There was never any encouragement. She was a doormat for Paige and Mia to wipe their feet on. And they did.

People would always say to my Twin, "Of course she loves you. She's your mother." But I gather those people didn't know the staggering statistics of infanticide. It is very possible for a woman to not love a child, and it happens more often than anyone cares to admit.

My Twin grew up with a hole in her heart. She became an expert at self-sabotage, and she didn't even know she was doing it. The opportunities presented themselves, but she was a door slammer. There were always people who wanted to love her, but she couldn't let them.

I couldn't help but remember a time when my Twin was in her twenties and she met the man of her dreams. It was a meeting out of a fairy tale. She was living in New York, and she and her friend frequented a quaint little restaurant on the Upper East Side in Manhattan. There was a waiter working there who was one of the most gorgeous men she had ever laid eyes on.

He was a tall man with engaging eyes. Even though he was working a busy shift, his uniform was still clean and he looked incredibly confident as he made his way through the dining room. One very tired night after dinner, he walked by their table and asked if he could get her anything else. She looked up into his gorgeous color-of-paradise blue eyes and said, "Yes, a pillow." He got down on his knee, and looking into her soul, he said, "I don't have a pillow, but you can use my shoulder." The next thing I knew, they were on his motorcycle, whisking through Central Park. My Twin was in heaven.

My Twin would spend many nights with him in his apartment while he played the piano, and she loved to hear him sing. He would even read to her from whatever book he was reading. She would lounge in front of the fire and write poetry. In the morning, she would wake up and do push-ups, and he would laugh. He told his brother that he had met his angel. And she believed it. She was his angel because he made her feel more beautiful than anyone had ever made her feel in her entire life.

Even though she was born there and knew the city well, she felt like a tourist seeing the Big Apple for the first time when she was with him. Everything was new and fresh, and all the sensations and sounds of the city were something that she was seeing for the first time when she was with him. She was so in love with him that if he walked into a room, she would know because she would become a klutz. She would drop things, knock things over, and blush. It was precious, and she had no idea how much he adored her.

But it was too good, and she thought she wasn't good enough. The love scared her, and of course she did the one thing her past had taught her; she left. The emotions were too strong, and she didn't have any frame of reference for such a happy and healthy situation. To her, the safest thing was to get out. To this day I know when my Twin thinks of him. She gets a little ache in the part of her heart where she keeps him.

She left the man of her dreams in one of her unconscious fits of transference. She was proving the Genius Mother right. She was her daughter, even if she didn't want her. Archangel Uriel showed up before I could call for him. I think my thinking of her lost love might have reminded her of him too.

> River skies and ancient waters, a moon-drip
> shadow never falters, loves lost are memory gains,
> a willful heart and stormy rains, all is young in
> timely innocence, a playful grin of effervescence,
> remember the laughter and me, feel the love and
> be free.
>
> —Age 32

My Twin didn't know what staying in a friendship meant until she was living in California again and one of the friends she made at the restaurant was a blonde girl named Faith who would become a fixture in her life. She tried not to be friends with her, but she saw right through my Twin. She was relentless. Faith was convinced that they were supposed to be friends. Finally, one day my Twin said, "Okay, I am going to tell you my story right now, and then I am going to walk away and not talk to you for two weeks, and we'll see how it goes."

Two weeks later, they were friends. Faith knew my Twin thought she was damaged, but she showed her that she could think she was damaged all day long, but she wasn't broken and was therefore fixable. Faith knew that Kate had wronged people, and she pointed out that the tears in my Twin's eyes while she spoke of it were proof that she wasn't a bad person; she just didn't know any better at the time. She pointed out all my Twin's good qualities and didn't let her forget them. She let her cry over how sorry she was for all the people she had hurt and for how much pain she felt over the people who had hurt her. She helped Kate find her light.

The more Kate found her light, the darker Paige and Mia became. Kate began to see how toxic her relationships truly were. It was as if her new friendship was lifting the layers of wool that Paige and Mia had pulled over my Twin's eyes. She was finally beginning to see that she deserved to be happy and that she deserved to have healthy relationships. Kate's feelings came up like a stubborn weed, and bitter, angry resentment fueled her hostility toward Paige.

My Twin wallowed in feelings of how Paige had ruined her life, but there was nothing she could do about it. And so the questions reared their ugly heads yet again: *How could Paige not love her daughter? Would the vicious cycle ever end?*

Then the call came. Paige was diagnosed with cancer. At first, Kate thought it was a joke or an exaggeration. But two and a half years later, my Twin sat in Paige's bedroom while she, skin hanging from her bones, preceded to talk her ears off.

Paige was a fraction of the woman she had once been. My Twin could vividly remember the anger and rage that had radiated at times from the woman who was her Genius Mother. But now Paige's skin was loose and sallow, the lights in the bedroom causing her to look a horrible shade of yellow. Large, dark blue bags hung under her eyes, and her thin face looked like a skull. A monitor near the bedside table beeped periodically, perhaps the only indicator that the Genius Mother was still alive. Her breathing was labored. With each word, she seemed to exhale a bit of her life.

She told Kate many things, some of which stood out for Kate, "I'm sorry I couldn't love you. You have to know your father was at one time an amazing man, and I was very much in love with him. I don't know if I ever stopped loving him. I helped push him away because I didn't know how to be loved or treat someone with love. You, Kate, are a miracle, and I am proud that you have grown into the woman you are in spite of everything you have been through."

As she sat there and watched her mother's body wither away like a flower left too long in a vase, she wanted to scream. She stared at the tubes and IVs, the various implements keeping her Genius Mother alive. When Kate tried to interject, Paige, raising her voice as much as she could through the cancer that had blocked her vocal chords, said, "Let me talk. I am the one on trial here."

She died six months later.

I watched Kate cry over her notebook as Archangel Uriel guided them both across their prospective pages.

It starts with a single droplet of water, like in a summer rain. I must surrender to the water's will. It comes out of nowhere and calls my name. My body responds voluntarily in surrender; the beckoning calls a much-needed release. As the water makes its claim on me, my body shakes for inner peace. Memories flood my mind as my steps I now retrace. The water flows freely and I yield to its embrace. An attempt at laughter, and I am at the point of no return. I freely relinquish all control and leave it to my heart to discern. It can start with an onion and the effects on the eyes, as I peel away at the layers I am left with no disguise. It can begin with a lullaby, sparking memories of the past. A childhood left to no one and praying the pain won't last. A remembrance of my Genius Mother—her singing fills my mind. A soul lost to happenstance who chose to leave this world behind. The grief from mistakes I've made fall around me like a house of cards, as I have spent most of my years, behind my self-made wall of disregard. The waves are finally crashing over me as my body relinquishes its control. Giving in to the convulsions of sobs, the only way I can be whole. In humility, I shall shed my tears, embracing all that they bear within. An inner knowledge and wisdom that only life experience can bring. Tears come in many forms, maybe too many to comprehend. But I am always thankful for the visit, like the comfort of a long-lost friend. Just as all the water from a rainstorm brings the gift of the brightest rainbow, I am always grateful

to my tears because I can see my life through their
open window.

—Age 33

Just when you think you have found your peace, the past
throws a wrench in your plan. So many people come from broken
homes or face tragedy at an early age. Some of us face both. How
is it that some people are crippled by it, while others rise above it?
I am now more than ever convinced that my Twin lived this life
because it was this life that brought her here. And here is where
she would be when the phone would ring, and against her better
judgment, she answered it.

The impending feeling of doom she would get when she was
up against something she couldn't do anything about came with
the sound of the first ring. And of course, the call brought news
that the life she knew was a lie.

It was Mia's voice on the other end as Kate suspected, and
she proceeded to tell her that rumor had it that Paige wasn't my
Twin's mother after all. Mia, the First Born, had received the truth
from what she called a reliable source. And while my Twin stared
at herself in her bathroom mirror, she listened to Mia's voice on
the phone explaining, "It was the Singer who gave birth to you."

Before she could go into detail, my Twin abruptly hung up
on her. Still looking in the mirror, my Twin said, "Let me get this
straight. I grew up in a household with the Genius Mother who
cringed at the sound of my voice and left me alone in a playpen
for the first three years of my life because she couldn't stand the
sight of me—and she wasn't even my real mother? My Aunt Janis,
who has said barely five words to me in over twenty years and
who quite possibly has multiple personalities, is really my mother?
Then who is my father? Did someone forget to tell me that I am

125

nothing but a character in a Nancy Drew novel? Is someone going to jump out and say, "You've been punked"?

My Twin's thoughts raced back to the days she had spent living with her Aunt Janis. She remembered not ever knowing whom she would be speaking to when she spent time with her. She remembered how unreliable the Singer could be. She didn't want anything to do with anyone who claimed to be a part of her family. At this point, she didn't really care who her real mother was, because it wasn't like either of the women—Paige or Janis—had ever really been a mother to her anyway. She also reminded herself how much Mia loved drama and chose to ignore the stupid accusations that made no sense at all.

But even so, my Twin's thoughts would get the best of her. All this nonsense threatened her intentions with disenchantment, sadness, and isolation. And then without introduction, the tears of a life gone awry came flooding out of her eyes. She cried hard and long. After numerous deep breaths, and while I held mine, my Twin looked into the mirror as the last tears rolled down her cheeks, and the angels began to speak to her through her thoughts.

"If we stay too long looking at our own reflection, we will start to see things that aren't really there. There won't always be someone to pull us out from behind the facade. What scares us the most is an illusion; it always was and always will be. Let bygones be bygones. Irony can get the best of you, and your imagination can lead you astray. But the world has a funny way of taking care of us sometimes. We don't always get it. What we want isn't always what we need, and what we think we need isn't always what we get. Remember the ancestral prayer sent to you from Howard Wills.

Ancestral Prayer

God, For Myself, My Spouse, All Our Family Members,
All Our Relationships, All Our Ancestors And All
Their Relationships Back Through All Time,
Through All Of Our Lives
God, Please Help Us All Forgive, Be Forgiven,
And All Forgive Ourselves Completely And Totally,
Now And Forever, Please God, Thank You God.
Lord, Fill Us All With Your Love And Give Us All
Complete Peace Now And Forever, Please God,
Thank You God.
God, We Thank You For Your Love, We Thank You
For Your Blessings, We Thank You For The Gift Of
Life And All The Many Gifts You Give Us Daily,
Thank You God, Thank You God, Thank You God
Amen.

Chapter 9
The Bridge

Yes, as you can imagine, the first half of my Twin's life left her breathless, subdued, and emotionally crippled. With no comedic reprieve, the stories were hard to read and the situations unfathomable. But I did tell you in the beginning that the events I would share were not the happy ones. And quite frankly, I don't know if I would have survived this.

However, my twin did. But little does she know, it's not over. I've watched her progress from an abused and troubled child into a grown woman, beautiful and strong, but not without her challenges; it's a testament to the love the angels bestowed upon her. Lighting her path, they guided her from her beginnings to where she is today. They have allowed me to see that the path of struggle can eventually lead to the path of enlightenment. And we hope hers does.

In the face of adversity lie many laugh lines. I see them now. As her life progressed, my Twin needed to know which lines to embrace and which ones to cover with makeup. But we all know that a cover up will wash away with a little soap and water.

Being the constant wonderer, it was inevitable that she would want to get to the crux of it all, and I had to ask the Archangels what this meant for the future. I must have blinked, because when

I opened my eyes I was standing in the Archangels' office, and they were all looking at me as if they were expecting me to say something, so I did "What?" I asked. "I came to you for answers." They laughed.

I looked long at our history and her feelings about it. Her wondering why helped her always reinvent herself. She had seen the consequences of each and every door she had ever walked through and the occasional window she jumped out of. My investigations into her behavior have proved the perfect paradox of wonder. My Twin should've had her heart hardened. She shouldn't have been able to let anyone in because she had never been shown love as a child. Against all odds, she made it through this part of her story. She heard the angels speak, and she is about to get tangible proof of their existence. So with a slight nudge from Archangel Uriel, she pulled out her notepad and started writing:

> Okay, Angels. I think you're here and that you can hear me. It it's possible, and I'm not crazy, I think you have been trying to teach me for most of my life. I am becoming pretty certain you helped me along the way. I believe everything happens for a reason, and if it weren't for everything that happened to me, I wouldn't be who I am. If you are there and you can hear me, you must be on this journey with me for a reason. I think it was in the many times of isolation that you worked the hardest to get through to me. It is time to right the wrongs and release the chains that bind me. This isn't just for me. It's for whoever else is listening.
>
> The compulsions to share, learn, and hypothesize about the events that make life better,

stronger, and sustainable is irrevocable. My story is far from over. But on this side of the water, across the bridge from where I came from, it sounds so much different.

I'm pretty sure it's because of you, my Archangels, that I survived it. Archangel Gabriel, you helped me when I couldn't help myself. Archangel Michael, you gave me courage when I was a coward. Archangel Zadkiel, you gave me strength when I was weak. Archangel Uriel, you held me when I cried, and you spoke to me of hope when I stared out into nothing. Archangel Rafael, you instilled in me undeniable faith. So am I done now?

—Age 35

Chapter 10

The Archangels

I found the archangels in their respective areas of the room, working diligently and quietly, but it was Archangel Gabriel who drew my attention. His hands were swinging vigorously in front of and slightly above him. The colors and images were visible again in the air like a 3D virtual reality experience. He was focused and precise, swiping left and right as if putting the images in order. It was like Stark from Marvel Comics, helped by Jarvis, building a master suit in his basement. Only Archangel Gabriel was laying out the master plan of my Twin's life. Was this the future we were seeing? I tried to get a better look and saw a time and place and people I didn't recognize. I saw my Twin at different ages and realized the archangels were right. It wasn't over; there was still much to unfold and quite possibly one more relationship that would test her strength and will. *Argh. Really?* I couldn't help but ask myself, *Will this ever end?*

One vision enthralled me not just with its colors and illusions but because it really was like watching a scene in a movie. It was obviously the future, and I was compelled to know more. The story was narrated in the distinct voices of the archangels, and I stood watching on the sidelines.

As the night fell on the ocean, bringing with it a sparkling, diamond-like shine to the water, the moon let us know my Twin was at it again. She was thinking too much. The thoughts were taking her into her past, where she hoped the answers were. The hopeless memories conflicted with her undeniable hope, mixed together like the cocktails she used to drink.

Kate sat upright in bed, her pen traveling feverishly, filling in the blank pages of her notepad. We tried to reach her, to be the conduit to the answers she sought.

Do you ever get the feeling that something is missing? And I don't mean just any old thing; I mean the possibility of someone who has been missing from your existence and there is no way for you to be made whole? Like someone took a rib or something, and it wasn't God or Adam? Like there was supposed to be another one of you, but somehow you got left behind?

There has always been this unequivocal sense that I was here for a bigger purpose, but I lost time by being my own worst dichotomy and giving in to the never-ending justifications of "why me?" I mean, how could you spend most of your childhood in turmoil without a reason for it? Maybe I was a mass murderer in a past life, and I was getting what I deserved. I sure as hell told myself that enough times over the years; how could I not start believing it?

How do you wake from that? How do you go from prey to hunter? How do you break free?

If we're lucky, one day we wake up and enough is enough. We start investigating on our own by looking back across the bridge from where we came. Something piques our interest, and we can't really tell anyone because "what will the neighbor's think?" and all that. But as the realization sets in that the signs were always there, it's time to take a good long look in the mirror. It's time to begin again.

The pen compels me to question my own impermanence. I must be a conduit. Things weren't falling apart, and it wasn't a slow progression or downward spiral. It was broken to begin with. The Genius Mother who gave birth to me could have sealed my fate, but something is telling me I was destined for something greater. Someone is trying to tell me I was better than the lies I was told. The memories are calling out to me in my meditations, poetry, and especially in my dreams.

And with that the pen fell from Kate's hand. With her heavy breathing came the sense that we were whirling through her mind. This time her dream took us back in time to a place long ago. As we both stood watching together in the coldness of the delivery room, I could feel all the Archangels with us chanting lightly over the buzz of the fluorescent lights and Paige's moaning.

My Twin was letting go. I could feel her fading away. I tried to hold on to her, but she slipped out of my grasp, and I couldn't hold her. As she left me, I could hear her promises that she would never leave me, but it made no sense. She was leaving me, and I had no choice but to come into this world without her.

With my first breath came her unmistakable voice. It was in my head, I think. It was quiet and whisper-like yet clear under my wailing as I tried to acclimate to the air and my lungs inhaled life for the first time. Who was my Doppelgänger talking to? The other voices were unrecognizable, and yet they seemed familiar. It was like a lullaby. Whispers masked by the sounds of wings softly brushing against the air.

Were those angels? I immediately stopped crying as I tried to listen closely to hear what they were saying.

"Help! Please help her. I couldn't do it. I wasn't strong enough to stay and help her. Oh, what have I done? How will she survive?" cried the Doppelgänger.

"Hush now," said the archangels. "It's all going to be okay. The dragon called upon us, so we knew she was coming. You weren't supposed to survive. We need you with us; you're the link. You are the only way for us to reach her. We have promised our protection."

"You did?" the Doppelgänger was confused.

"Yes, and there is much for you to know, but for now we will just say this: There will be times when you will want to turn your head and cover your eyes, so just do it. Look away and trust that we will hold her through the most arduous times. Be prepared that in your connection with her, there will be times when you feel what she feels, and it won't feel good. There will be times when you will want to grab her and take cover, but you can't. Also know there will be times when she will know laughter, but that isn't what this story is about. And most importantly, you cannot interfere with what happens to her. She must live out these events so she may one day know her purpose."

"Dragon?" She screamed as she opened her eyes. Drenched in sweat, she saw the clock read 3:45 a.m., and my Twin realized she was in bed. "Oh, that dream again," she muttered as her head crashed back down onto her pillow. But as we watched, her thoughts flooded back to her as if she had never slept.

Staring up at the ceiling, she wondered if all the soul searching was finally getting to her. She whispered, "Maybe I should stop all this writing. This may be bigger than my mind can fathom." But just as fast as the thought formed, it evaporated, and she knew as well as we did that not writing wasn't an option.

Her thoughts were proof that we were getting through to her. I could hear her thinking, "I know it sounds crazy, but someone is trying to tell me something, and this is the only way they can reach me."

Little did she know it, but her poems of yesterday were soon to become her epiphanies of tomorrow. So her pen found the next blank page in her notepad and went to work as her clock clicked over to 4:00 a.m.

> Riding the pendulum like a crescent moon, I find the faith in what must be coming soon. I push forward like a swing and don't hold back. The gravity comes for me and I don't react. Just ride the wave of this vibrational level. An uplifting monument to the road less traveled. Thankful for times shared and lessons learned. Live with integrity and leave no stone unturned. It has simply become my own narration. An exercise of will and a worldly translation. A language that speaks to all of us. Truthful in nature and one we all possess. Open your heart to the innocence of the beauty in sharing unconditional love.
>
> —Age 36

In the vision, the alarm sounded in her ear. In my reality, the fog rolled in behind the windows. I couldn't help but be reminded of how often she let herself be blinded by the density. Living with your head in a cocoon is challenging when you are trying to break free of whatever has its hold on you. How do you let go of things in zero visibility when you can't see in front of you? In the surrender, she gained some answers to some very old questions, and just like that, was reintroduced to the beauty and power of the archangels. But she wasn't quite convinced. Not yet.

To me, the memories all make sense now. The messages were loud and clear. In the darkest moments of her youth, they were the lightning bugs that lit the sky. They saved her life when it threatened to take her. They sang her to sleep with lullabies of optimism and expectation.

Even though she couldn't see the archangels then, she will see them soon, if Archangel Gabriel's visions are correct.

Once upon a time, she had landed on what she thought was a permanent seat on life's proverbial roller coaster. The Band-Aids had piled up for so long that she couldn't tell which bruises were healed and which needed tending to. With the help of her team of archangels and me, I'd like to think, she will attempt to rip them all off. What lies underneath will be proof that the next part of her journey has only just begun and that her karmic debt isn't finished being paid, so there's still more to come.

Archangel Gabriel looked away from his work and spoke to me.

"We are the chosen guardians in your Twin's story. We will pick up where you left off telling her story, since it is time for us to make our presence known to her. We have been given permission to show ourselves, and show ourselves we will. We are to be her saviors, bringing her across the bridge of what her life once was and into what it is meant to be".

"Hopefully we can still reach her in time," Archangel Zadkiel added.

"Oh, we will", replied Archangel Uriel as he quickly grabbed another scroll and lead Kate through another poem of hope and assurances.

There are moments that are precious, and daytimes that are still. A knight in shining armor, a game of strength and will. Let your sword of enlightenment enter me with faith. Embrace my body, mind, and soul with elegance and grace. Impress upon my darkest dreams the laughter of a child. Innocence will heal all wounds and dress thee with a smile. If ever I forget these words, cast your light on me. So I may witness the beauty in everything I see. May I never turn a blind eye on that which I don't know. Yesterday's mistakes shall be my victories of tomorrow.

—Age 36

Kate's life had been a roller coaster riddled with challenges, and the negativity had many moments of victory. But as promised when this journey began, I wouldn't give up hope that together we would persevere.

While on a shoot in Los Angeles, a colleague recommended a book to Kate about angels written by Doreen Virtue. The book sounded beautiful and intriguing, but at the time, my Twin just wasn't ready.

About a year after the conversation when things in Kate's life were starting to spiral out of control again, she gave herself over completely, asking for help or a sign or anything that would encourage her. Then she waited. She deliberately silenced herself. She didn't force it. She believed, implicitly, that help was near. The next day while snooping around online for an uplifting book to read, there was the page with the Doreen Virtue book that her colleague had told her about. In utter excitement (but not knowing why) she downloaded the audio books, and the meditations and submersed herself in the theories, the possibilities, and the love.

Her life began to undergo a transformation. The signs were everywhere, the messages were clear, and her sense of self started to show signs of restoration.

One day while on her favorite hike, which has a labyrinth-style maze at the top of the climb, my Twin got into her place of intention, and she walked the maze. Since it was a journey she was embarking on with her angel guides, it was only fitting that she brought them with her. "Angels, thank you for always being by my side. Thank you for guiding me. Please continue to envelop me with your light so I will know peace. Please guide me toward the people and tools that will help me heal my past and make way for a new future. Please help me cut the umbilical cord from where I come from and please give me the strength to stop repeating my past. Please give me indications that I am on my right path. This I ask in gratitude. Thank you."

Not long after her hike, while reading *The 12 Keys*, by David M. Friedlander, my Twin was reminded of the magic of manifestation. The encouraging stories of Bill Gates, Jim Carrey, Steve Jobs, and Oprah were reminders of people just like her who had persevered.

She kept a little money plant on her desk, and one night before she went to bed, she put it in the sink to give it some water. She got in bed and drifted off to sleep with a smile on her face and an angel meditation in her ears. With a silent, love-filled prayer, she drifted off.

Upon rising in the morning, she grabbed her coffee from the kitchen, and on her way to her desk, she remembered to grab her little plant from the sink. At first she couldn't believe her eyes, but then she remembered she had asked the angels for a sign. One of the leaves on her little plant was in the shape of a heart! She took pictures. She would post them with a write-up on the new blog site she was creating. Proof that she was not alone, that none of us are, would be the push she needed to take the leap into the Angels' arms.

But it doesn't mean the challenges will cease to exist. No, those will just keep coming. The path set forth by the karmic debt of times past still has a balance owed, and we will help her finish out the payment plan that sealed her fate by Lord Hadrian's hand.

The Karma Chronicles Part 2 Archangel Interventions, coming summer of 2018.

The Karma Chronicles Part 3 The Lord and His Dragon, in development.